KILLER'S CREEK

It was named Killer's Creek when a child was killed in a fire. Henry Walton took the blame, instead of Doctor Rudge's wayward son, Jerry. Henry, when he was forced to leave Stillwater, formed a travelling circus. But Jerry Rudge reappeared in Chaparral, Utah, bringing trouble . . . The fire destroyed the rolling stock and Henry had to sell out. He rode the vengeance trail to Stillwater. Nothing could stop this lethal clash, or prevent Killer's Creek claiming a second victim.

Books by David Bingley
in the Linford Western Library:

THE BEAUCLERC BRAND
ROGUE'S REMITTANCE
STOLEN STAR
BRIGAND'S BOUNTY
TROUBLESHOOTER ON TRIAL
GREENHORN GORGE
RUSTLERS' MOON
SUNSET SHOWDOWN
TENDERFOOT TRAIL BOSS
HANGTOWN HEIRESS
HELLIONS' HIDEAWAY
THE JUDGE'S TERRITORY
KILLERS' CANYON
SIX-SHOOTER JUNCTION
THE DIAMOND KID
RED ROCK RENEGADES
HELLIONS AT LARGE
BUZZARD'S BREED
REDMAN RANGE
LAWMAN'S LAMENT
THE COYOTE KIDS
BRIGAND'S BLADE
SILVER CREEK TRAIL
OWLHOOT BANDITS

DAVID BINGLEY

KILLER'S CREEK

Complete and Unabridged

LINFORD
Leicester

First published in Great Britain in 1969

First Linford Edition
published 2009

British Library CIP Data

Bingley, David, *1920–*
Killer's creek - - (Linford western library)
1. Western stories.
2. Large type books.
I. Title II. Series
823.9′14–dc22

ISBN 978–1–84782–734–0

Published by
F. A. Thorpe (Publishing)
Anstey, Leicestershire

Set by Words & Graphics Ltd.
Anstey, Leicestershire
Printed and bound in Great Britain by
T. J. International Ltd., Padstow, Cornwall

This book is printed on acid-free paper

1

The small cowtown of Chaparral was situated in the south-west of Utah territory. Had it been located a few miles farther south it would have been in Arizona. A similar distance east and the state of Colorado would have claimed it. It was a place of little consequence, having a population amounting only to a mere few hundred.

Around three in the afternoon, those whose work kept them in town were mostly dozing, following the habit of *siesta*. But this particular day was different. Walton's Wonderful Wild West Circus was in town, and young Henry Walton, the proprietor, had gambled a little by billing the first performance at the tail end of *siesta* time.

In the evening, the performance needed a lot of lit lamps to make it go, and Henry had a secret fear of fire and what it could do to a packed circus tent. This sort of catastrophe had never occurred in the short time during which he had run his circus, but that did not minimise the fear.

When the show was about three-quarters finished, Henry hovered by the animal entrance, gnawing thoughtfully on a matchstick. His fine brows were raised and he did not need to be told that the show had been a success.

As always, Bella Lester was drawing a lot of applause from the men who were watching. She was on the 'high' wire, though the size of the tent meant that the drop beneath the wire was never more than ten or twelve feet. Henry liked to give his customers spectacle, but nevertheless he was glad that Bella would never fall from a great height.

His pulse registered excitement as the two-thirds-full marquee marked the girl's talented performance with prolonged 'ohs' and heartfelt 'ahs'. There was a brief hush while she contrived a 'fall', catching her weight behind a bent knee and circling back into the upright position.

Bella danced off the wire and took her bow, while the audience yelled, cheered and clapped their applause.

Henry sighed with relief. Two men, who had also been watching with a professional interest, left the other side of the entrance and approached Henry. The little man, no more than four-and-a-half feet tall, was billed as Muchachito. His birth certificate intimated that he was Isaac Bird. He was more familiarly known as Little Ike.

Little Ike swung on the arm of the other, older man. Bill Trask, in his early fifties, could give the dwarf twenty years. He had greying, thinning hair and a limp, but his enthusiasm matched that of the younger man.

'Doggone it, Henry,' Bill enthused, 'there was a time when I used to have my doubts about young Bella goin' on that wire, but she's mastered it like she masters every-thin' else she turns her hand to! I guess you must be proud of her, same as we all are!'

Henry glanced across at Bill, transferred his gaze to Little Ike, and finally blushed. 'Sure, sure I'm proud of her! Wouldn't any circus man be that way?'

Without waiting for an answer, he ran forward and caught Bella as she hurried to leave the ring. While Sam Juarez, the Mexican, played an extra roll on the drums, Henry presented Bella to the folks all over again and drew from them an extra round of applause, given ungrudgingly.

Then, side by side, the pair withdrew from the audience's view, and Little Ike entered the ring to take Bella's place, pushing a coloured ball almost as big as himself. The paying customers roared with delight while four men, hired locally, took down the apparatus connected with the balancing wire.

Henry and Bella pulled up short, outside the marquee.

They looked at each other.

The girl was twenty-two years of age. She was five feet four inches tall, and extremely shapely and fit. Her long straight black hair was parted down the middle and tied back at the nape of her neck in a ribbon. A certain something twinkled far back in the wide-set green eyes and tiny patches of vivid colour tipped the high cheekbones as she looked into Henry's face.

'Was — was it all right?' she asked, her voice intimating a possibility of doubt.

This was her way of keeping the relationship between Henry and herself strictly a professional one. He realised this all the time, and winced at her question.

'You know darned well, Bella, that it was good, very good! You don't have to be all that modest, especially in front of me, anyways! I've always appreciated what you've done for the show, an' never more than right now!'

Henry relaxed his strong grip upon her hand. Bella touched her bosom, above the fluffy silk outfit which was scarcely big enough for modesty. She glanced down at the long black tights which sheathed her legs, and wondered for perhaps the millionth time exactly what Henry thought of her.

He looked as if he was going to say something of a more personal nature, and at once she was embarrassed.

'You'd best get ready to take the hosses in, Henry. It wouldn't do to keep the folks waitin 'on the first performance!'

Henry accepted the mild rebuke. He intimated that he would talk to her when the show was over. Already he was dressed in the fringed buckskin outfit which he normally wore when he paraded the six highly trained horses in the ring. He watched Bella mount the steps to her wagon some thirty yards away, and then stepped inside a small canvas room which served as a rest place for the artiste waiting to perform.

On the wall was a mirror and brushes and a comb.

He hauled off the wide-brimmed dun hat and glanced at himself. Tiny crowsfeet wrinkles at the outer end of his steady blue eyes made him look a trifle older than his twenty-five years. His short, crisp, fair hair was almost sandy in places. He had regular features, and a strong nose and jaw.

In spite of his private doubts, he looked and was the absolute master of the small outfit which he had started. He combed his hair and made sure that his appearance was all that it should be.

As soon as he was ready, he stepped out into the open and gave a faint whistle. The palomino, which was his own private riding horse, snickered in the corral on the far side of the circus sprawl. There was a pounding of hooves, and two rather unkempt local hands came hurrying across the open ground holding three lead ropes apiece.

Along with the palomino were two blacks, two whites and a sorrel mare. All of them were well bred. Henry had bought them one at a time, when he could afford them, and a good deal of his off-duty time had been spent in training them. He had animals in his blood. This gift he had inherited from his father, who had started adult life in a livery and followed it up by becoming an animal doctor.

Henry was happy working among animals, although he knew certain disappointments in his life which kept him from being as contented as he might be.

He talked easily and soothingly to the six spritely animals which were suddenly about him. The hired hands were dismissed as he led the horses to the ring and removed the lead ropes. Little Ike ran through them as they came in, and the audience, waiting expectantly, sent up a round of applause for the sleek appearance of the quadrupeds.

Henry ran into the middle of the ring, doffed his big hat and cracked the whip, which he only ever used for guidance. He felt the audience with him, and began his act.

* * *

Ten minutes later, Bella had slipped out of her tights and balancing rig. Instead she was clambering into a man's checked shirt, tailored denim trousers, and a white stetson which had set Henry back a few dollars. She assured herself that the shirt and pants were fitting decently and placed the hat on her head. It came down over her ears, and brought a ready smile to the mobile mouth.

She snatched the hat off again, fixed her raven black hair closer to her head and drew over it a golden blonde wig. When the lighter hair was in place, the hat fitted well. She was checking herself over in the mirror again when somebody knocked softly on the tailboard of the wagon.

The girl caught at her breath, though she was in no way scared.

'Ike? Little Ike? Is that you teasin' me again? 'Cause if it is I'm goin' to have to do somethin' about you, you hear me?'

There was no reply to her query. After a few seconds, a man cleared his throat and the knock was repeated.

'Who is it?' Bella demanded.

'An admirer, ma'am,' a slightly husky voice informed her.

'Well, lands sakes, admirer, you sure do pick a funny time to do your admirin'. Jest what exactly did you have in mind?'

Again, the man was slow to answer. Bella's curiosity got the better of her. She crossed to the rear end of the wagon and pulled back the puckered curtain. The face of the tall young man standing beneath her was half in shadow. All she could really see were two seemingly bloodshot eyes in a face half hidden behind a handsome brown moustache of large proportions.

The fellow touched his hat, a black one with a stiff brim, and pinched in at the crown.

'The hair is a different colour an' you've changed, but I believe you to be the same young lady who recently entertained us on the high wire. Am I right?'

'Why, yes, you're right,' Bella admitted hastily, 'but I have to go into the ring again in a minute or two. I can't rightly stay here an' talk with you, sir.'

'Let me step into the wagon while you sign your autograph for me,' he suggested eagerly. 'Will you do that, an' no more?'

His persistence was beginning to annoy Bella. She always liked to be within easy distance of the ring for a few minutes before she went into it. This fellow was frittering her time away. She almost sent him off, and then relented. Perhaps it was a curious feeling about his husky voice which made her yield.

'Oh, very well, then. If that's definitely *all* you want, you can step inside. I have a pencil right here, if that will do?'

His breath smelled of strong liquor, but he clambered into the wagon without effort and sat himself behind the big trunk directly inside the tailgate. Bella pushed an old hand-bill towards him, and raised her brows in a silent query about its suitability.

'Sure enough, that'll do, miss.'

She let out a long breath, simulating patience which she did not really feel, and lifted the pencil. With a flourish, she wrote her name, Bella Lester, and added the words 'best wishes'. The admirer shrugged his shoulders more firmly into his dark tailored jacket. He lifted the paper and peered more closely at it.

'Bella Lester, eh? Well, it ain't the name I expected, but it's interestin' jest the same! Doggone it, Bella, but you look jest as fetchin' in that blonde wig as you do with your own hair down!'

He chuckled rather wickedly and held out a hand towards her, but she backed out of reach, covering her mouth with her fingers. In this last utterance the stranger was no longer husky voiced. He had spoken clearly, and she knew him, in spite of the growth of moustache which shielded his handsome features, and the rather cynical expression.

She almost choked. 'Jeremy! Jerry

Rudge, in the flesh! An' you dare to come into my wagon an' make out you're an admirer of mine! How could you do it? Have you no conscience at all?'

Rudge casually pulled a short cigar out of his vest pocket and stuck it between his lips. Clearly he had been drinking, but he knew what he was doing. He did not attempt to light the cigar.

'Is it a crime to admire a pretty lady, Bella? Is your memory so short? I've always admired you — you remember how it was back in Stillwater? Well, don't you?'

Bella appeared to have wilted. She leaned against the frame of the wagon for support. Another roar of applause carried easily from the marquee, but it had no effect on the pair in the wagon.

'You gave me a surprise when you signed your name. I'd have thought it would have been Bella Moran, an' not Lester. But maybe your marriage to Moran didn't work out, an' you don't want to be reminded of it!'

From the depths of despair, Bella began to find spirit in her again. This man was taunting her, seeing how far he could rile her. And she knew him of old. Moreover, he was taking liberties, saying these things in the privacy of her wagon. His father would never have allowed him to behave in this way towards her.

'Get out of my wagon, Jerry, an' don't come this way again, hear me?'

He shifted the cigar around his mouth. 'Is that a threat, Bella? What are you aimin' to do with me, if I don't obey you?'

Rudge came to his feet, staggered slightly and recovered himself. He raised a boot, as though preparing to step out at the rear of the wagon. At the last moment, he changed his mind and lurched towards her, catching her by the shoulders and causing the pair of them to clatter up against the side canvas.

Bella was breathlessly trying to fight him off, whereas he was simply resting his weight on her, and laughing into her neck, blowing her with his whisky breath.

'Let go of me,' she protested, struggling hard.

'Give me a kiss, for old time's sake, Bella.'

Rudge tightened his grip and swung her around, but the girl tripped him and caused him to crack his head against a metal stanchion. That changed the expression on his face. In spite of the many small obstacles littering the wagon bed, they fought and swayed over its full length before Bella's breathing grew harsher.

Rudge was only about eighteen months older than her. He was strong and determined to humiliate her. Suddenly she changed her tactics. She filled her lungs and was about to shout. Rudge divined her purpose, but did not wholly stop her mouth.

She got out: 'Henry!'

The hand closed over her mouth. She regretted not having had time to don her ornamental spurs, but her boot toes cracked against his shins a couple of times before he wore her down still further. For a few seconds neither of them noticed the tail curtain open.

Henry Walton hurled himself at them like one of his own wild cats. He tore them apart without making much allowance for the weaker person. Two short arm jabs in Rudge's ribs severely curtailed the clash and enabled him to manoeuvre the intruder towards the door. Rudge resisted when he came to the steps. In avoiding a vicious swing, however, he temporarily lost his balance, and a backhanded blow sent him all the way to the ground.

'Get right away, mister, an' don't come back — unless you want me to prefer charges against you! What you've jest done don't find favour with real men! Not in Western courts, anyways!'

Rudge got up and crouched, fingering his jaw. 'All right, Walton, I'm goin' now, but you ain't heard the last of me! I'll be back an' when I come I shan't give any warnin'. That — that girl can look out, too! She ain't no Lester, she's a Moran, an' you both know it, so help me! You both think you've got the world by the shirt tails, but you ain't!'

Henry watched Rudge go. He then turned and stood stiffly just inside the wagon gate, his brows raised in enquiry.

Bella swallowed hard. 'Sure, I'm okay, Henry. An' I'll be along for the target shootin' in jest a moment. So go along an' break out the guns, will you?'

Henry waited a few seconds more, murmured an apology of sorts, and then did as she had suggested. That performance, his revolver shooting, was only average, and that of Bella was clearly moderate. And still the crowd sympathised with her. Carrying out the usual routine, Henry had the palomino and the sorrel mare run out after the evening meal.

Although she didn't feel like exercise, Bella sided him in the ride. They rode a mile and a half out of town, and then backtracked. All that way, they said nothing to each other. Fifty yards from the circus site, they pulled up.

'You realise the intruder was Jerry Rudge, don't you, Bella?' Henry asked, rather stiffly.

'I could hardly fail to notice that, seein' as how I was raised in Doc Rudge's house, Henry,' the girl murmured.

She shook her reins impatiently, but something in Henry's manner held her back.

He said with an effort: 'There's somethin' I'd like to tell you.'

'What is it, then?'

'You remember the reason why I left Stillwater?'

Bella felt herself tighten up inside. She remembered all too clearly the tragic incident to which Henry was referring. She found it hard to speak of it, even after three years.

'You mean about what happened to the little Mex girl when the shack was burned down?'

She recollected how Henry, who had

been camping near, had been found trying unsuccessfully to put out the flames in the burning dwelling.

He nodded. 'I wanted you to know that I didn't set fire to the shack. All I did was try to put it out. I'd like for you to believe me, if you could, Bella.'

Obviously, Henry didn't expect her to believe him straight away, because he kneed the palomino and left her behind. He left her very thoughtful, and wondering why he had chosen this night of all nights to make such a revelation to her.

It had to be the unexpected clash with Jerry Rudge, another resident in distant Stillwater, New Mexico territory. Bella felt better after hearing what Henry had had to say, but she was still puzzled. Suspicion of having fired the building had fallen on Henry, and he had allowed himself to be named the guilty party.

He had left Stillwater shortly afterwards, and never made any point of going back there to deny his guilt. All the same, the Mexican child could scarcely have set fire to its own home. Burning brands from a fire had been found in two or three spots near by. If Henry was innocent, had he been sheltering the guilty party all this time? The unwanted clash with Doc Rudge's wayward son was pushed into the back of Bella's mind as she pondered privately over the new puzzle.

2

Walton's wonderful Wild West Circus packed a whole lot of worthwhile entertainment for its size. It was so small that every capable performer was really a star. It had started in a small way through Henry's having been banished from his home town.

When he left home, he felt the parting, and to make up for the loss of friends, he turned to an old love which he had shared with his father, since deceased; that of animals, and their care and training.

At first it had just been one horse. Then he performed with two, and then three. Bill Trask, already fifty years of age, and down on his luck when a similar outfit folded, was the first real trouper to team up with Henry. Bill also had the love of animals. In his time, he had trained dogs, wild cats, horses and bears, and he it was who encouraged Henry to think big, and to expand.

Bill was also a first-class handyman, and he doubled as the first clown with a face which looked as though it had been fashioned especially for grotesque make-up.

Little Ike joined them some three months later, as they toured the south-west and worked to pay their way. Ike needed the circus. He could not easily fit into an ordinary outfit owing to his lack of inches. He was just as determined a worker as Bill, his speciality being knife-throwing. He also worked in comedy scenes with Bill, and helped out with the horses. Furthermore, he was absolutely fearless when it came to handling big cats and the bear.

A long spell at a mining camp enabled Henry to build up his stock and equipment, but the outfit didn't really begin to make its name until Bella popped up along the route. Bill and Ike perceived from the start that Henry and Bella had known each other in the past, and known each other well. These more experienced troupers managed to get the young man and the girl over the stiff, almost hostile part of their first meeting.

Eventually, when Bella explained that she was a widow and looking for work, Henry offered to take her on. She jumped at the chance, although she was far from easy in his presence alone. She worked for her keep only, at first, and then for a small wage, which was increased from time to time.

Relations between Henry and Bella eased a little. Both found that they could tolerate each other provided that they always stuck to the circus business and kept from talking about the past.

Like Ike and Bill, Bella was soon worth her weight in gold. She was gentle and effeminate, and yet she had a strong will and a determination handed down from her pioneering ancestry which would have graced many a powerful man.

She worked with the horses and did

all manner of odd jobs, while she practised with guns, firing against the target and taking tuition from Henry. Soon the target shooting became a double act, and she was pestering him to obtain the necessary apparatus for a high-wire act.

At the time when Jerry Rudge erupted back into their lives, Bella had only been on the wire for a few weeks, and all the regulars were concerned about her. This concern was also reflected in the faces and mien of Sam Juarez, his wife Juanita, their two lumpy girls and the bright-eyed small boy who conducted patrons to their seats.

The Juarez family completed the retinue, apart from casual labour hired at each new town.

* * *

Poor Henry could not clear his mind of the threats which Rudge had uttered just before he left in disgrace. Young Walton had good reason to know how bad an enemy Rudge could be, and how vulnerable a circus could be if anyone sought to tamper with it. He personally checked all the cages, and saw that all the equipment was properly stacked away for the night, much to the disgust of Ike and Bill, who slipped away to confer with Juarez.

Bella had made no mention of the invasion of her privacy, and Henry had also kept it to himself. The latter's brow was furrowed when he sought out his three key men and offered them the price of a few beers.

His shoulder was against the side of the bear's cage when he opened up his mind to them. 'Boys, I'd like for you to go along into town an' slake your thirst. Only don't stay too long. Durin' this afternoon's performance a man came along an' made a nuisance of himself. He also issued certain threats which I don't intend to take lightly. I don't reckon the local law would take easily to guardin' a circus, so I'm askin' you to come back an' relieve me when you've had a reasonable quantity of beer. Think you can back me?'

'Do you have to query such a thing, Henry?' Bill asked, shaking his head. 'We knew you had somethin' troublin' you afore the show closed.'

Juarez raised his palms to the sky. He then tilted his fingers downwards in a polite but formal gesture. 'In thees sort of beesiness, Boss, your troubles are ours. We will help. I will tell José, as well. He hears everything, but *everything*! Most embarrassing!'

The weight of responsibility lifted a little as Henry thought of Sam's bright-eyed boy hearing all the most intimate utterances between his parents.

Ike's high-pitched voice cut in. 'You want I should sleep in the grizzly's cage, Boss?'

Bill chuckled. Henry said: 'Ain't no use in teasin' a bear of that size, Ike. If he took a fancy to you, you'd hardly make him a worthwhile meal!'

In this way, the watching problem

was settled. Henry had wanted to ask the men to keep a special watch on Bella's wagon, but he knew that they did that already, and that they would have been embarrassed to have it mentioned.

Henry took three glasses of beer himself, after the trio had returned. He drank them in different saloons, and although he looked most closely around the gambling tables and long bars he saw no further signs of Jerry Rudge. Once over, he was tempted to slip into the hotel and take a look at the register, but he fought down the inclination and tried to keep things in proportion.

After all, Jerry had been drinking before he made his untimely attack on Bella. He was just as likely sleeping it off right now, and many a drunken man regretted his talk and behaviour when no longer under the influence. Such thoughts finally sent Henry to his roll in the first wagon. He slept fitfully until about one hour before dawn.

At that time, sleep slipped away from

him, and the cause was nothing to do with the cold temperature. He had a distinct feeling that something was wrong. Without disturbing Bill, who shared the sleeping quarters with him, he hurriedly slipped into his trail clothes and picked up a whip and a lariat.

The setback he feared most was the liberation of the wild animals. He put this before his fear of fire, which was substantial. Soon, he was catfooting across the vacant lots towards the animal cages in a pair of worn mocassins.

The big grizzly grunted and snuffled in the privacy of its huge cage. Henry sighed with relief. The sigh was scarcely out of him when he saw a ghostly figure flit across his vision some twenty yards away. His heart lurched. One of the cats was out. He thought he knew which one it was, too, and although it was making for the main street of Chaparral, he hastened to the cages and checked the locks on the doors.

The three female cats were all in there. Something had disturbed them, but they were all in their places. The door of Khan's cage, however, swung soundlessly on well-oiled hinges. Henry felt his mouth go dry.

A sound came from the wagon he had vacated.

'Henry?'

'Khan's loose. Stay around here, Bill. Keep a close watch!'

'I'm a-comin'.'

'Stay right here an' watch,' Henry repeated.

He hurried across the vacant lots and was just coming out into shadowy Main Street when his senses were assailed by an almost inhuman cry some fifty yards away. A body slumped on boards and further startled the circus boss. He was assuming Khan had caused that cry, and he was not far wrong. The tiger's tail had brushed the face of a fat drunk, sleeping off the effects of his liquor on a sidewalk bench. The noise was when the fellow hit the boards.

Heavy breathing drew Henry up the street. He moved quietly, every now and again calling the tiger by name, and using one or two Indian words which its first keeper had taught it. There was another burst of sound on the night air. Somebody came out of a building beyond the drunk. Henry hastened on by the frightened man, whispering that he had nothing to fear.

'I *saw* that tiger, it wasn't the drink workin'. I saw his big baleful eyes, an' he looked right into my soul! I — I don't know why I'm still alive now.'

The Town Marshal, his shirt tail still flapping outside his pants, was close enough to hear what the drunk had said. The lawman croaked and then groaned. He thought that chasing up a slinking wild animal in the middle of the night was beyond a joke; especially for a man whose eyes were a little past their best for night vision.

Henry kept ahead of the lawman, not wanting to stop and explain. They were on opposite sides of the street, and moving fast for that time of the night. As it was, the lawman was the first to see sign of the beast. Two glowing coals of eyes faced him. Behind them the sloping back just fitted under the batwing doors of a saloon.

The big cat sniffed and pawed the boards, twitching his tail restlessly. The Marshal thumbed back the hammer of his gun, and Henry heard. At once, the circus man backtracked and got between the lawman and the animal. He called to Khan once by name, and at once sent the rawhide loop after him. It settled over his neck. Khan tried to wriggle loose, but he heard the crack of the trainer's whip, and that settled him.

Behind Henry, the Marshal began to shake as though he had contracted ague. His gun hand was unsteady, and his lower jaw shook as he tried to ask how the beast had escaped.

'Marshal, it's hard to explain. There was nothin' wrong with the door of his cage, an' no carelessness. I'd say somebody released him for a dare, or for a poor joke. I don't reckon it'll happen again. In any case, I've alerted my staff. We can't afford to lose a tiger as valuable as this.'

'Maybe it'd be as well if you kept this business to yourself,' the Marshal opined, after a long pause.

He was beginning to think how things would appear to the townsfolk who elected him into office. Henry was in a similar frame of mind.

'My sentiments entirely. I'd take it as a favour if you'd say nothin' about it. I sure would like to lay hands on the hombre who opened the cage door, though.'

They parted and went their separate ways. Henry said the same thing to Bill when he got back, about the cage opener.

'Sure thing, Boss,' Bill replied. 'An' the jasper who paid him to do it.'

Henry's brows shot up in the early dawn. He decided that Bill had a specially perceptive mind. The man they might be looking for would be a coward, most likely. One who would arrange for another to do his dirty work.

3

In spite of his disturbed sleep, Henry perked up after breakfast and a long confidential talk with Bill Trask. The latter had pointed out that it did no good to sit back and wait for trouble. A man had to show potential enemies that he was capable of looking after his own property.

Henry thought about the Town Marshal who had so nearly shot a vital animal. He decided not to let the matter of the released tiger rest there. After the first meal of the day, he made a slow tour of the wagons and the cages. In the marquee, Bella was practising the most difficult part of her high-wire act. He nodded to her and grinned rather sheepishly before telling all in earshot that he was going into town for a short while on business.

The second saloon he called in was

called the Prairie Dog. Even at that time, when the sun was scarcely giving out its accustomed heat, there were drinkers and talkers. Henry wandered about. In the gloom of the large room, dressed in ordinary trail garb, not many men would have picked him out as the circus proprietor. He wanted to keep it that way while his ears worked for him.

In his first saloon, he had drawn a blank. He had not been clear what he was listening for at that stage. He had gravitated around half the groups in the Prairie Dog when it occurred to him that he ought to be listening for a man who had suddenly come into a few useful dollars.

He was going to be lucky this time. Around the corner of the long bar were three nondescript drinkers, bellied up close. Each of them wore ordinary trail clothes. They did not appear to spend much of their incomes on soap, or in barber shops.

Henry rested a foot on the rail, and contemplated his beer from a mere few feet away. Something in his appearance made the ugliest of the trio raise his voice and talk more loudly. For a minute or two, the circus man brooded over this sudden change. Had the fellow identified him as Walton, or was he merely a show-off, a man who had to talk big in front of a stranger?

He had almost made up his mind that the fellow was merely a natural-born big-mouth when the subject of the talk crowded out the other conjecture. The man was talking about the circus, or about circuses in general.

Henry listened hard and well, and studied the fellow's reflection in the long mirror. The talker was a thick-set man in his late thirties. His fleshy face was pockmarked, and quite a time had elapsed since it last made contact with a razor. Tousled brown stubble camouflaged the lower part of the face and to some extent hid the fleshiness. His hat had a broken brim. His shirt and vest were shabby.

Just as Henry finished summing him

up, the man threw a second golden eagle, worth ten dollars, on to the bar. The trio watched it spin and catch some of the light from the nearest lamp. Its owner flattened it on the bar with a bunch of stubby fingers.

He chuckled and called for another round of drinks. His companions made a fuss of him, seeing as he was doing all the buying. He cleared his throat, filled his lungs, and began his recital again.

'Like I was sayin', boys, them big cats, they ain't all that difficult to handle. All you have to do is let them see who is master. You keep an eye on 'em an' crack the whip now an' again. Above all, don't show 'em no favours, see?'

Henry's pulse quickened. Without knowing it, his mouth had formed into a hard line. He was fully aware of what he was doing when he started to nod, very decidedly, at what he could hear from the loud-mouthed drinker.

Here was a man who didn't appear to work too often; one who had money and who was keen to show it. Moreover, he was talking about circuses and seeking to convince his friends that he had once worked with a circus and doubled for the animal trainer on occasion. Here was the type of man who might summon up sufficient courage to sneak into a circus layout and open the tiger's cage door before slipping off again. A man who was a sufficiently irresponsible bum to grab a fast and easily-earned dollar.

The circus owner began to cultivate him. With little moves, easily identified as approval of the continuing talk, the listener formed an invisible link with his victim. The talker, Den Rollins, appeared to grow in stature as he provided the entertainment.

After a while, Henry yawned. He cleared his throat while the trio were still drinking. 'Say, would you gents like a drink at my expense before I move on?'

The pair who were not paying were not particularly interested. They felt sure that Rollins would pay for all they needed during that drinking session. Rollins himself reacted differently. He suddenly tired of his two hangers-on.

'I reckon I'd like to drink with you, mister, but I was thinkin' of changin' to another bar. Would you care to accompany me?'

'Doggone it, I surely would, friend. Let's go find ourselves another long bar to lean on! It helps now and again to change the beer a man drinks.'

Rollins gave his friends an elaborate wave. He fell into step beside Henry and emerged from the building, brushing back one side of the flapping doors with his chest. Henry stopped, hesitated and started down the sidewalk rather slowly. He paused for Rollins to catch up.

'Amigo, you have a certain look about you. I reckon you could look one of them wild cats down at the circus straight in the eye! You could stare it down, even if it was ravenous with hunger, an' the beast would back off first. I have that feelin' about you, an' I don't get to feelin' that way any too often these days!'

Rollins gasped with pleasure. Even then it did not occur to him that he was talking with the master of the outfit. He gulped and grinned, draping an arm around Henry's shoulders. Like that they advanced for another five yards. A man who had been lounging in the shade near the end of the false front stepped down into the dust and crossed over. This unplanned move prompted Henry to spring a surprise upon his suspect.

Rollins replied, 'Say, you're a very discernin' feller, mister. Fancy you bein' able to tell about my talent with animals when you'd only seen me for a few minutes in a bar! It sure is true, though. I could do jest about every-thin' with cats, apart from makin' 'em talk. Why, if they was short of a trainer down at the circus I'd go along right now an' take over!'

Henry scanned the boards on either

side of the street and decided that there was no one near enough to take particular attention over what he planned. At the first alley, he grabbed Rollins by the vest and hustled him into the narrow shaded space.

Rollins blustered. 'Why, what's the idea, amigo?'

'I'm lookin' for a man who ain't afraid of tigers. A man who's jest been paid a few more dollars than he usually has in his pocket. A man who's feelin' pretty important over what he had to do for the dollars! *You* fit the description, Mister Den Rollins, an' I think you can tell me a whole lot of useful information! You never told me anythin' worth while while you were soundin' off in the bar back there, except that you were an empty-headed braggart!'

Instead of begging him to talk, Henry hauled back his right fist and planted it on the angle of the unshaven jaw without more ado. Rollins banged against the wooden wall behind him.

He looked angry. At the same time, he seemed as if he was trying to assess Henry's ability with his fists.

'You must be mad, stranger! An' to think I came out of my way to drink with you!'

Henry telegraphed a second punch, a left this time. He started it on its way to the side of the man's head, then changed direction and thumped him hard in the chest. Rollins doubled over.

'I think you are the man who opened the cage of the male tiger an hour or so before dawn,' Henry murmured. 'Every second that ticks by makes me more certain of that, too! By now you ought to be wonderin' why I'm specially interested!'

He grabbed his victim by the throat, twisting the soiled bandanna a little, and helping to hoist him upright.

'I — I know you now,' Rollins admitted. 'You're the owner, Walton. There's somethin' about your eyes.'

'Who paid you to turn the tiger loose, Rollins?'

Henry kept his voice quiet, but there was a deadliness about it which was hard to describe. Rollins kept up his protestations just a few seconds longer.

'Surely you can't really think I let that big Bengal tiger loose jest because I was talkin' about circuses an' cats?'

Henry's face was just inches away from the frightened man's as the grip on the bandanna tightened a little more. 'Did *I* say it was a Bengal tiger? I don't remember sayin' that!'

'All right! All right, so a man paid me to do it. He said he was acquainted with the trainer an' wanted to play a joke on him.'

'Describe the man! *Pronto!*'

Rollins' eyes rolled a little, so that Henry had to slacken his grip. Quite suddenly, the latter saw himself and the fracas in the alley as a bystander might have seen it. He pulled away a little.

'He — he was a tall man. Maybe your height, I'd say. I met him jest for a minute or two about eleven o'clock last night in the private room of the Broken Wheel. He put it to me bluntly, an' paid me in advance. Said he'd know if I didn't do a good job, an' he looked real mean when he said it, too.'

'What did he look like, apart from bein' tall?' Henry prompted.

'A big brown moustache, he had, an' a hard face with a funny way of smilin' an' big brows, an' a big black hat an' a jacket the same colour. Is that enough? What do you aim to do?'

Henry released his grip and Rollins sagged against the wall. 'I intend to make sure it doesn't happen again, that's all!'

He gave Rollins a last piercing look, and started towards the mouth of the alley. As an afterthought, he turned on his heel and threw two bits towards the other.

'I hope the beer sours your stomach, Rollins!'

The cage opener sagged against the wall, sucking in breath and ignoring his tormentor.

* * *

Fifteen minutes later, Henry drank a beer at the bar of the Broken Wheel. He looked the place over and saw that it had a balcony and extra rooms. When the barman had drunk beer at his expense, he asked the important question.

'I'm lookin' for a man named Rudge. Jerry Rudge. I believe he was doin' a spot of card playin' in your private room yesterday evenin'. Is there anyone in the back room now? I don't see my contact in here.'

The balding barman stopped polishing glasses and peered around the lofty room. He took his time over it, and went away to serve another customer before telling Henry what he wanted to know. Meanwhile, a well-dressed man, who had been drinking farther along the bar, detached himself from his friends and went out by a rear door.

Another couple of minutes went by. The barman came back. He appeared to remember Henry's query. It brought a grin to his lips.

'Oh, yes, you was askin' about the back room. Why don't you go on over there an' look for yourself? It wouldn't do any harm if you didn't disturb the players!'

Henry grinned and nodded. He made for the door which the barman had indicated. He knocked and stepped inside. It was smaller than he had anticipated, and it had another door in an adjacent wall. Seated at the table were four card players. Jerry Rudge was one of them, and judging by his expression he didn't appear to have been winning. He was, however, on the alert.

He remarked, 'Something I can do for you, stranger?'

Henry nodded, and wondered rather hurriedly what he could do about this type of reception. One of the quartet was a professional gambler in a hard derby hat. Another was a big-time rancher. The third was well dressed, but mean-looking and nervy.

While Rudge awaited an answer, one of the other players blew his nose. A second one yawned, and the third looked pointedly at the intruder and gave the impression he would like to have him thrown out for interrupting.

'There's nothin' you can do right now, mister. I wanted to tell you that a fellow claimed to have taken money from you in this very same room for doin' some mischief at the circus. I wanted you to know I knew about it, an' that your little effort didn't come to anythin'!'

Rudge acted the part of one baffled. 'I didn't part with any ready dinero to anyone last night, mister. Or this mornin', either. As a matter of fact, I can get rid of it easily enough in this card game!'

One of the other players chuckled. Henry surmised that Rudge had touched on the truth there.

'Did you say this hombre parted with money yesterday, in *this* room?' the professional gambler asked.

'I didn't say yesterday, but the time stated was eleven o'clock. Nearly midnight. I suppose you're goin' to tell me that was impossible now?'

The gambler nodded very decidedly, losing a half-inch of ash from his cigar. 'At that time present company were all playing hard. Nobody came in at that time. An' what you say couldn't have happened later, because we didn't leave the room all night. Fact is, we fell asleep in here, an' we took breakfast in here before we started up again.'

The rancher added, 'I was a-sleepin' across that door you came in by. You're makin' a mistake, stranger, an' wastin' our valuable playin' time.'

There was a threat behind the rancher's words, and the nervous man with the smouldering eyes suddenly felt like adjusting his revolver in the holster.

'You see how it is, stranger,' Rudge pointed out, sneering openly.

'I do,' Henry returned firmly. 'But Den Rollins ain't the type to leave town in a hurry. Don't go too far, is all.'

After nodding to the table in general, Henry backed out without undue haste. At the bar, he took another drink, wondering who had been through ahead of him to tip off the gamblers about his presence. He didn't stay long enough to find out.

4

Bella had been more disturbed than Henry thought by the events of the previous day. While he was still in town investigating the matter of the released jungle cat, she suddenly tired of her practising and asked Sam Juarez to bring out the sorrel for her.

Sam knew that it was never her habit to ride in the morning. He thought of saying that it might leave the mare out of sorts for the afternoon performance; but Bella never forgot about the welfare of the animals. Even if she was troubled, she would not overwork the beautiful mare.

Sam was standing by her wagon when she emerged in her denims and shirt, adjusting her hat.

'If Henry comes in an' asks where I am, tell him I jest went off for a short change of scenery, Sam. I guess he'll understand.'

'Okay, okay, I'll feex it with him, Señorita Bella. But don't be away too long, will you?'

The girl favoured him with her most fetching smile and deliberately walked the mare off the lots and into Second Street. She worked her way through the town and took the opposite direction to the one Henry had selected for their earlier rides.

As the buildings dropped behind, so did the buzz of human voices. Bella revelled in the solitude for a while, and then tired of it. She had walked the sorrel almost a mile when the idea came to her that she would like to turn off-trail and take a look at the surrounding country from higher ground.

Such a move would make a distracting change when she could not gallop her mount unduly. Fifty yards farther along she saw a gap between outcrops on the north side of the track and decided that the slope behind the gap would suit her purpose admirably. She checked the mare's forward progress until it was scarcely moving and stared at the low barrier of scrub on the trail side.

Just as she had selected the place where the mare would have to go through she heard human voices. They came from the spot which she had just selected for her observation. She halted the mare, which tossed its tail and glanced around at her, as though it were politely asking if she knew what she wanted to do.

The voices went on. They were speaking in short rapid bursts of American and Spanish. Bella surmised correctly that one or both were Mexicans. Instead of turning off the trail at that spot, she urged the mare forward again and kept going for almost another half-mile.

She had not any reason to think that the men hidden from her view might be hostile, but following the occurrence of the previous day her nerves were jumpy. She started to make excuses for herself. If the mare had gone through the scrub it might have scratched its hide, and scratches were unsightly in a circus ring.

The minor occurrence had shown

her that she was still anticipating trouble, either for Henry, or for herself. She did not like the feeling.

* * *

Alonso, a bandy-legged, middle-aged Mexican with a cast in one eye, flicked one of his spur wheels with a long twig. At the same time, he nodded his head and felt the swing of the upturned brim of his steeple hat. His partner, a swarthy Texican with a perpetual frown on his long face, made a mouth noise registering disapproval.

When Alonso ignored him, the Texican said: 'I tell you he won't come! We ought to have been on our feet when that rider went through jest now. We could have taken him for his roll an' been back in town in half an hour. Nobody would have missed us!'

Alonso spat. His spittle sizzled in hot dust.

'You are a fool, amigo. I tell you the *Americano* will come!'

‘*Why* will he come? An’ how can you be so sure, eh? Tell me that!’

‘He’ll come because nothin’ happened with the other man. You recollect when he sent us away, he’d set on that other fellow? Well, this is over half a day later. The man in the saloon was an impatient person, one with a big grudge. He wouldn’t wait this long. An’ up until the time when we left town, nothin’ had happened except what the drunk was talkin’ about, an’ nobody seemed to believe him. I asked one of the helpers at the circus an’ he couldn’t confirm what the hombre was saying. So, I tell you again, the *Americano* will come!’

Heath, the Texican, aimed to spit out tobacco juice. He was careless enough to lose his chew of tobacco at the same time. This put him in an even worse humour. Even the sound of the big horse coming along from town at speed almost failed to restore his spirits.

Rudge called out hoarsely. Alonso at once replied, and gave minute instructions about getting through the scrub and the outcrops. Heath was soon on his feet and taking the sweating dun into his care, but it was Alonso who first took the newcomer's attention.

'So, you came like you said you would,' Rudge remarked, as he worked on his face and neck with a kerchief.

'I think you knew we would come, *señor*,' Alonso retorted. 'It is you who are late, if anyone.'

'I was delayed. Anybody been here while you were waitin'?'

Heath perceived that their would-be employer was in a slightly jumpy mood. 'If you mean right here, the answer's no. On the other hand, there was a rider went through ahead of you a short while ago.'

Rudge glared into first one face and then the other. He began: 'It wasn't anyone from the — '

'It's very unlikely that anyone would come this far at this time from the circus, seein' as how they have a performance this afternoon.'

The little Mexican had been the one

to cut in, and to anticipate what Rudge was going to say. Rudge nodded. He sat down rather heavily on a hot rock and felt the heat go through his clothing. He also felt the wad of folding money which he had to hand over to get his present assignment under way.

He neither liked the look of these two men, nor did he relish their smell. They were unclean, and seemingly unaware of it. He could not imagine more unsavoury allies than these to whom he was to surrender his reserve of money, the wad which he had kept sewn in the lining of his jacket for a very long time.

'This will be the first and last time we shall meet,' he pointed out. 'I shall pay you before I leave here, an' you will have to start movin' right away. On no account are you ever to recognise me again. Is that understood?'

Alonso and Heath nodded rather solemnly.

'Exactly what is it you want done?' the latter asked impatiently.

'What I have in mind won't be easy,'

Rudge admitted. 'Therefore, I'm prepared to pay you accordingly. Now listen, an' listen good . . . '

He talked for about three minutes, then stopped. Alonso asked two questions, and Heath professed himself satisfied. The latter was counting the bunch of treasury notes while Rudge shifted his weight rather hurriedly from one foot to the other and yearned to be on his way.

Alonso cleared his throat and glanced away to where the dun was cropping yellowed grass. Rather grudgingly, Heath went off to collect it. Rudge was quick to swing a leg across the saddle. He had a last word or two to utter before he moved off.

'You, in the steeple hat. Get rid of that headgear before you approach the outfit. Understand? It'll draw too much attention if you're seen!'

Alonso nodded. Rudge had gone up a little in his estimation. The brief delay while the dun was collected had a bearing on what ensued, for Bella on the mare went past the same spot before Rudge got out into the open. By standing in his stirrups and pushing the dun forward a couple of yards, he was just able to see the mare and its handsome rider.

A change came over his cynical features. He turned with a triumphant leer on his face. 'For your information, that rider who went through earlier is jest goin' back again. It was a person from the circus, too!'

For the first time since the meeting started, Alonso lost a little of his calm. Rudge let him perspire before assuring him that he would take care of that side of the business himself.

* * *

Bella was almost a furlong nearer town by the time Rudge's mount emerged on the trail and began to come after her. As soon as she heard its hooves and the jingle of harness, she turned in the saddle and took a good look at the rider. She had no reason to associate the dun with Rudge, of course, but he was wearing the same hat and coat as when he had visited her the previous day.

He kept his head down and covered his moustache with his hand, but even then the girl was very suspicious. Her heart started to thump with excitement. She felt she ought to keep well out of his way, if it was Rudge again, but that would mean galloping the mare and it wouldn't be good for her.

Perhaps if she just kept the animal at a fast walk she could keep ahead. Another glance, two minutes later, confirmed that it was indeed Rudge. She shuddered and gave herself over to wonderment about the place where he had shown up. It was exactly the same location as she had chosen for herself when she wanted to go off-trail and take a look around.

She found herself wondering if he could read thoughts; whether he was some truly evil genius who could direct the lives of those whom he intended as his victims. Was he one of the two men she had heard talking earlier?

At first she had little reason to think otherwise, but soon she noticed that the dun had been ridden hard and quite recently. It seemed that he had come out from town not very long ago. Perhaps there had been three men through the outcrop, after all.

Rudge rowelled the dun unmercifully. He knew that he had lost face in his encounter of the previous day, and he wanted a chance to make up for it. He called out hoarsely to the girl, marvelled that she did not force the mare to an equally fast turn of speed, and gradually overtook her.

'It was good of you to wait for me, Bella,' he began breathlessly, as the dun came up alongside the mare.

One furious glare from her angry green eyes made it clear that she did not relish his company.

'You showed me all the nastiness you had in you yesterday, Jerry. I wonder you have sufficient nerve to seek me out again, after that! In any case, what's the idea?'

Rudge shook his head and blinked away salty perspiration.

'Bella, you'll never ever believe it, but this meetin' was a pure accident! I had no idea you were out ridin' this way, no idea at all. But I do feel pleased to have met you again. You'll recollect I was the worse for liquor yesterday when I invaded your wagon. I wouldn't have done it, otherwise. Not in any circumstances. Besides, you're a married woman. Ain't you?'

There was a short, painful silence, during which mare and horse paced along side by side. Rudge asked the same question again.

'If you must know, I'm a widow, but I don't want to discuss it,' Bella admitted, tentatively.

Rudge allowed a minute to elapse before his next question. 'Pardon me for askin', but is it a long time since Moran died?'

'Quite a long time.' Bella sounded bitter.

Intrigued, Rudge went on: 'So you didn't have a lot of married life, after all?'

'A mere matter of an hour or two was all.'

The listener tried in vain to hide his curiosity. Bella did nothing at all to help him. Presently, he reminded her that they used to live under the same roof, that, in a way, she owed something to him because his father had raised her.

He went on: 'If you'd jest tell me what really happened I wouldn't have to keep on askin' question after question. Would I, now?'

'I agree with you when you say I owe somethin' to your father. The fact is, Moran didn't desert me, as you're probably thinkin'. Within a very short time of the actual marriage, I heard him talking to some old cronies of his. They were plannin' a raid on some place to come up with easy money.

'As soon as I realised he was workin'

outside the law, I picked up a few things, begged a lift out of town an' never saw him any more!'

This revelation kept the questioner quiet for another minute. He lit a small cigar before he continued the painful interrogation.

'Are you sure you're a widow, Bella? I mean, if you never saw him any more, how do you know?'

She turned on Rudge with the full force of her bitterness. He could see that she loathed him, but he still needed an answer to his last question. He was a man who could take a whole lot of loathing and not be really hurt.

'All right, you want every sordid little detail, so I'll tell you! I didn't have to see him again. I read about him in a newspaper! He was shot, gunned down by peace officers when he was tryin' to make a getaway! *That's* how I know I'm a widow, an' I don't feel any better about it for havin' to tell you, either!'

The way her breasts heaved against the shirt intrigued Rudge. If what she had told him was true, then her marriage had never been consummated. He thought about this and decided that she was more desirable than ever. He began what he thought was a more subtle approach.

'This — this marriage setback. It must have unsettled you, Bella. You ought to try again. Put Moran and the past behind you. You're the marryin' type, all right. I could see that as soon as I spotted you on that high wire the other day. Now, take me, I'm the marryin' type, as well. Moreover, my Pa has money. He makes me an allowance.

'If you could see fit to adjust your ideas about me I could be good for you. Now, what do you say? Is it worth a trial?'

While he had been leading up to this, Bella had been calculating the distance still to be covered to town. It wasn't far. Just as Rudge was leaning out to put an arm around her, she lashed out with a gloved hand and caught him across the face. He pulled back, wincing, and before he could recover, she had asked the mare for a gallop and got it.

The sorrel extended itself. A hundred yards before the first buildings showed up, Rudge gave up the pursuit, knowing that he would cut a bad figure, bringing up the rear when there was obvious bad feeling between the two of them. Bella realised that he had stopped hunting her. She slowed down, and had reassumed a modicum of her usual poise by the time she was negotiating the first street.

Bill and Sam came to meet her. She slipped to the ground, admitted to them that she had not been able to forgo just a little gallop, and begged them to give the sorrel a careful grooming before Henry saw her.

These two men were her willing servants. So was Little Ike, but he saw her when she was in the wagon, thinking no one could see her at all. From underneath another wagon some thirty yards away, he saw her take out from her valise a sheath knife. She extracted the knife most carefully from the sheath, and tested the blade against the ball of her thumb. As soon as she was satisfied with it, she replaced it in the sheath and went to some trouble to fasten the belt and sheath around her waist, inside the waistband of her denims.

Ike wondered about this unusual act, and about the galloped mare. He decided quite rightly that Miss Bella had troubles. After mulling over what they might be, he rolled out from his resting place and went in search of Bill. Many years had elapsed since Bill's rodeo days. He didn't look very formidable, especially in clown's makeup; but he was still a man to reckon with.

It wouldn't do any harm to tell Trask what he had noticed.

5

The circus started its second performance in Chaparral without incident. The acts started in a polished though modest way and gradually increased in appeal. The big grizzly made its appearance and set the men in a good humour. Many of them had hunted such animals, and they appreciated the skill and courage needed to deal with and train them.

A comedy act succeeded the bear, and then the cats were in the ring. During their act, the man who had had his drunken sleep disturbed kept shouting out that Khan was the one that had nearly eaten him. No one took him very seriously. They put his talk down to hallucinations and returned their attention to the ring, and more clowning.

Bill Trask, in full clown's make-up,

ably assisted by Little Ike, kept the comedy going with surpassing skill, knowing just how far to prolong the act without losing its point. Finally, he glanced out of the ring and received a nod from Henry, who wanted the next act on.

Bella was to follow on her high wire. Henry always tensed before she appeared. He could not help it and the seasoned troupers sympathised with him. A rush of feet went by as the helpers appeared with the special apparatus and the wire itself.

Henry watched every move they made. That was one time when the audience did not need to be entertained. They knew what was being rigged and they chattered away to each other, keyed up with anticipation. When everything was in place, Sam Juarez nodded, and Henry stepped forward and tested the wire for tautness by tapping it with a long pole.

At length he was satisfied. Sam dashed off to herald the new artiste with an introductory blast on his trumpet. The notes were still hovering on the air when Bella came alongside of Henry, looking fresh and keen and bright-eyed. He held her back for a moment.

'Bella, is everythin' all right with you?'

His probing blue eyes seemed to take in every little detail of her face. He seemed more intense than usual. She wondered if it was because of Jerry Rudge and the previous day's scene. Obviously, he was asking because of that. She nodded, and then smiled. It was a big smile, the kind she usually kept back until she was in the ring with the eyes of the audience closely focused on her.

'Sure, Henry, I'm okay! I won't let you down!'

As soon as she had said this, she saw a hurt look come into his eyes and she regretted the flippant answer. He had been really concerned about her, and not her performance. She wanted to say more, to make her answer sound a little more personal; to show more feeling. But Little Ike and Bill were moving forward, seeking to usher her towards the ring.

Henry cleared his throat and nodded. He took her by the hand, trotted with her into the ring, and joined her in a bow while the welcoming applause flowed over them. As he straightened up, the crowd quietened expectantly. Bella had been talked about since the previous day. Great things were expected of her.

'Ladies an' gentlemen,' Henry began, in his loud ring voice. 'This circus is proud to present to you the one and only Queen of the High Wire, the West's own Bella Lester!'

This time Bella bowed on her own. Henry withdrew, all the while watching her climbing to the height of the wire. Bill Trask came up behind the owner and pushed into his mouth a lighted smoke. Henry hastily adjusted his lips around it, and then thanked the older man without turning away. Bella took her time and went through all the preliminaries, moving backwards and forwards and using the gay parasol for balance and colour.

The audience liked and admired her, and from time to time, when she was resting on one of the platforms above the ladders, they clapped and seemed to be encouraging her to more daring deeds.

Everything went well until the girl was due to fake her 'fall'. She did the rehearsed slip, but as her bent leg wrapped itself around the wire, something slipped. At the end where the tightening handle was something had moved. Henry gasped. Bill lost his smoke, and Ike ground his teeth. The audience was not quite sure whether she had intended what she did or not.

Bella made a big effort to come upright on the slackened wire, but owing to the lack of tension in it she failed. She did another awkward circle on it, not knowing quite how to finish off. At the same time, Henry dashed forward until he was under her.

'All right, Bella, break it off!'

He crouched underneath, his legs bent at the knees, his arms extended upwards to catch her, hoping that the audience would think it was all part of the act. Bella, unfortunately, had skinned the back of her knee and also the palm of one hand. She slipped away from the wire rather awkwardly.

Henry had to shift his position almost at the last second. Consequently, the girl landed on him rather heavily. An elbow caught him directly below his breastbone and drove the air out of his lungs in a very painful fashion. He folded under her and at the same time cracked his head on a supporting stanchion. Bella's senses slipped away at the same time, and almost a minute of absolute silence went by, apart from the patter put out by Bill and Ike and Sam as they carried the limp pair out of the ring.

This was an occasion for extra

comedy, while the wire was removed. The audience applauded a brave attempt by the clowns to make light of the way Bella had downed her boss, but the accident had unsettled the paying customers.

Juanita Juarez, Sam's wife, bathed Bella's face, neck and temples in a small alcove until she recovered her senses. After blinking hard for a few seconds and examining her hand and leg, Bella opened her mouth to ask about Henry.

'Don't worry, *señorita*, he will be all right. Just now he is feeling very sorry for himself because you knocked all the wind out of him, an' when it is done with such force it takes a little time for the lungs to fill again.'

Second later, Henry appeared. He was bareheaded and walking rather unsteadily. A wet cloth, which he had clutched tightly in one hand, helped to keep his senses clear.

He was still breathing rather harshly when he said: 'Bella, take it easy. You don't have to appear again this performance. They can do without you.'

She laid a hand on his arm, this time letting him see that she appreciated his concern over her. 'You're the one who took the beatin', Henry, so don't you go botherin' about me. I'll be on my way to the wagon an' get ready for the shootin'. I guess the folks won't hoot if I ain't too good at the target practice today, eh?'

Seeing that she was determined to go on, Henry changed his tactics. Instead of trying to get her to pack up for the day, he delayed her, explaining that with the extra comedy everything would be running a little on the late side. To this she agreed, sharing a small wooden bench with him.

Henry remarked: 'I guess the folks back in Stillwater sure would be surprised if they knew what we did for a livin' an' could see us both now!'

Bella wrinkled her nose and became thoughtful. 'You're darned tootin', Henry. Especially old Doc Rudge!'

Their glances met at the mention of the doctor. Henry sighed, and Bella briefly squeezed his hand. He was about to reply that they could both do with a little attention from the doctor, but his thoughts kept slipping away to young Jerry, the sawbones' wayward son.

This brief harmonious sojourn was rudely terminated by the one word which could always be guaranteed to throw Henry into a panic.

'Fire!'

Henry gripped Bella by the forearms. Together they rose to their feet. Henry found himself muttering something about the harshness of fate in a manner totally foreign to him in ordinary times. He thought about the possibility of panic, and drew Bella out into the open, intending to silence the person who had shouted, in the event that the fire was not threatening circus property.

They ran a yard or two clear of the marquee, fascinated by a harsh crackling sound and a long streamer of smoke. Khan roared from his cage in sudden fear. His females took up the protest, and the grizzly added his raucous baritone. The burning was all too close for comfort.

'My wagon, Henry! Surely Jerry Rudge couldn't have done that to me?'

She looked away from the sorry sight, as though seeking solace in her companion's eyes.

'If you'd gone over there when you wanted to, it might have prevented the fire. On the other hand, you might have been trapped inside! I'm glad you didn't go!'

'What can we do?'

Bella peered around desperately. The circus always had to depend upon the settlements it visited for its water supply and firefighting equipment.

'Go back into the marquee, Bella! Tell the boys to keep the show goin' if they can, an' to announce that the audience are in no danger! An' send any of the local hands over to help me. I must try an' get the animals' cages out of the fire area!'

'I wish you luck, Henry! Don't take any personal risks!'

Bella slipped away, and Henry went a little closer to the blaze, trying to assess a useful course of action. It was difficult to think clearly owing to the fierce crackling and the oppressive heat. The upper part of Bella's wagon, the canvas cover, in fact, was a blazing pyre. The cries of the trapped animals, whose cages were directly in line with the blaze, were renewed.

The rest of the town was gradually becoming alerted to the danger. Men ran across the lots from Main Street and Second Street and the nearest intersection. Henry raised his arms, determined to use the townsmen to some purpose, even before the firefighting started.

'You men come on over here an' lend a hand, will you? This burnin' wagon is threatenin' two others!'

His cry for help stopped those who were sightseers and not helpers by nature. Henry made for the shafts, and when it was seen that he did not seriously burn himself, four men masked their faces and lent a hand. Others joined them when a rope was found, which could be secured to the shafts. Slowly and gradually, they turned it out of line and started to move it down a slight slope to a place of greater safety.

It gathered momentum, but just as it seemed that their efforts would be successful, a slight hollow in the ground sent it off balance. The rocking motion was enough to remove the burning top, which fell across the tongue of the Juarezes' wagon. A side of Bella's wagon blew out, and that was a signal for the helpers to withdraw in disgust.

The performance was over by that time, and the audience had streamed out of the marquee and withdrawn to a safer distance to watch the conflagration. Henry despaired of ever saving anything. The Mexican family's wagon burned every bit as quickly as Bella's had.

A party under the Town Marshal had appeared with buckets. They formed a chain from the town pump and passed the water from hand to hand, using the first dozen or so of bucketsful to dowse the remaining wagons and the beasts' cages. The splashing water frightened the trapped beasts as much as the fire peril. It was to the animals' cages that Henry then turned his attention.

The faces of some of his casual labourers floated before him out of the sea of heads and the swirling smoke.

'We'll have to draw the cages away from the area!' he bellowed. 'You could best help by assistin' me with the shaft hosses! Leave the firefightin' to the townsmen for now!'

It was a testing time for everybody. Two of his helpers went off to join the bucket brigade, not fancying being close to the cages with the horses. Another pair, however, although mildly singed already, moved across to the temporary corral with him and quickly secured three horses. They were restless as the harness was thrown across them, but the men were determined.

Henry went off with the first one to the cage of the big grizzly. By that time, the scared animal was thumping his feet on the bed of the cage and, for a change, thumping the roof with his head and shoulders. The whole cage was rocking. The owner thought how much better off he would have been if this powerful animal had been in the shafts.

The harness horse, a full-barrelled grey, refused to go anywhere near the shafts. He feared the bear, the advent of fire, the shouting, hurrying men and the sounds of splashing water. Henry bullied and coaxed, all to no avail. He turned over the halter to a bystander and tried to help the other two men. Neither of them had any better luck.

No ordinary harness horse was going into any shafts on that spare ground that day. The watchers, jostled nearer the cages by the line of bucket swingers, began to close in on Henry and his struggling assistants.

A man shouted, 'It ain't right, leavin' them beasts in there when they're scared half to death by the fire! They ought to be out!'

A hook-nosed, big-eared deputy pushed his way forward, biting his underlip, and trying to think what was best to do.

'Mister! Mister Walton, I think that feller who shouted was right! We'll have to have the animals away! Don't you agree?'

'An' if we can't shift the wagons, Deputy, what then?'

Henry, to his own surprise, was acting with great restraint. He knew he was in danger of losing his whole outfit, and still he was keeping what he hoped was a sense of proportion. His late father, an animal doctor, would have sided with the man who had shouted. The initiative was his, Henry Walton's, this far. He didn't want to lose it, either.

'All right, Deputy. I'll act on that suggestion. But it will mean shootin' valuable animals. I won't tell you how valuable they are! Maybe you can keep some sort of control over these sightseers, if I make a move.'

The deputy nodded and hurriedly backed away. He started to explain to those who were prepared to listen what was about to happen.

Out of nowhere, Little Ike showed up with Henry's heaviest rifle. He handed it over, his face working with emotion. Bill Trask's horny hand rested momentarily on Henry's shoulder.

'The grizzly will have to go first,' Henry shouted. 'He'd leave a gory trail if he got the chance, in a situation like this!'

The more daring of the sightseers appeared to have split up. Two crescents formed near the cages of the tigers. Not many ventured near the grizzly's spot. Henry checked over the weapon and stepped closer.

He called over his shoulder: 'You two had better stand by the cat cages, I guess!'

He sensed rather than saw his men move away. He stepped a little closer to the cage of the grizzly, which was still acting as though it was in a frenzy. Its tiny eyes glowed momentarily in reflected firelight. Henry lined up the gun, licked his lips and squeezed the trigger.

The animal roared, shook its head, stepped back a pace, still holding the nearside bars, and then slowly folded until it was an inert heap on the cage floor. Men who had been afraid to go near now crowded forward, coming between rifleman and victim.

Ike came around the edge of the new crowd and gripped Henry's arm.

'All right, Ike, I'm comin' as fast as I can!'

'Boss! Boss! Somebody's there before us! The door's open!'

Henry arched his brows, for a few seconds unable to comprehend Ike's statement, and then he was all action. He saw a clear space between himself and Khan's cage. He moved rapidly with spare shells jingling in his side pocket. He watched for the lithe body of the Bengal tiger to emerge.

The door shook. Khan delayed his leap. Henry fired, missed by a hair's breadth and cursed himself. Khan appeared to change direction in the air. He shot away towards Henry's own wagon and hid underneath it, while the assembled men roared with excitement and called from their midst those who had been thoughtful enough to bring shoulder weapons with them.

In the back of Henry's mind, one man's voice registered, but he took no notice of it. At the cage of the female cats, he had better luck. One of them succumbed to his first shot while Bill struggled with the lock which was hard to manipulate.

The door opened suddenly, causing the second shot merely to burn another cat. In seconds the cage was empty. Two guns roared in the direction of Khan's escape. Somebody shouted in triumph. Men scattered, moving faster than they had done in years, as the sleek, frightened cats bounded through them.

The firing of three or four shoulder weapons was redoubled and raucous voices told of another killing. When his animals, the live ones, were no longer in sight, Henry gravitated towards his wagon. He was in time to see Jerry Rudge coming away from it with a smoking gun in his hands. Rudge's was the voice he had heard earlier.

Others were pulling the tiger out from under the wagon, tail first, which almost certainly meant it was dead. Henry felt and looked lost, but, seeing him, Rudge flinched away a few steps before finding his courage again and calling for his fellow gunmen to take up the chase of the one cat which had escaped unscathed.

Henry hovered between the empty cages and the two burning wagons.

A voice which he knew extremely well said at his elbow, 'Henry, do you think Jerry Rudge hates me enough to set fire to my wagon?'

He cleared his dry throat. 'It's hard to say, Bella. One thing you can be sure of. He has an outsize capacity for hatred!'

6

That quick succession of damaging setbacks had left poor Henry in such a grim, morose mood that when flames licked the upper sagging canvas of the marquee, he was slow to respond. He had already written off his outfit as a rolling circus, and he thought that he was past caring.

Ike, Bill, Sam and Bella, however, all rallied around him and urged him to turn his attention to the big tent, which they had always thought of as the big top.

'Doggone it, Henry, you ain't a beaten man, not yet,' Bill protested. 'The flames over there certainly look bad, but there's items inside the tent well worth the effort of savin' them!'

'Any humans in there?' Henry asked, without enthusiasm.

'You know you care about all those

fittings in there you've jest been renewin',' Bella argued. 'Even if this show folds up, you'll be able to start out again. It ain't like you to give in!'

Bill glared at him and went off to collect the biggest axe. Ike, not waiting for his return, started towards the customers' entrance. Bella, with her hand on Henry's arm, felt the muscles ripple in it. He was going to fight again. Pushing her aside, he hastened after Ike and caught up with him by the swinging canvas flap.

'All right, so I'll see what I can do, but you, Ike, an' anybody else who shows up here has to stay by the door, an' that's an order!'

Ike glared. He changed direction, going under Henry's arm. Once inside, he glanced up at the burning canvas. Henry, following him, did the same. The fire had a good hold, and the canvas was too high to throw water on it. Ike started to collect up small, useful items which could be salvaged. Bill appeared with the axe, and Henry forgot about enforcing the rule of keeping others out. He snatched the axe for his own use, and ran into the ring, under the highest part of the marquee.

'If I could chop down one or both of these longest poles, the canvas would flop, an' maybe we could stamp it out on the ground!'

'Might be worth a try,' Bill yelled back. 'I'll see if I can find another axe anywhere!'

Henry loosened his buckskin jacket and threw off his hat. He tested the weight of his tool and swung it against the post. The blade was sharp. It dug deeply into the seasoned wood. He withdrew it, swung it, and tried again. Smoke billowed down towards him as he worked.

He was vaguely aware of the others, coming and going with small useful fittings, otherwise all his strength and concentration was on the job in hand. The breath came and went from his open mouth as he toiled. After some five minutes or so the pole parted and half the tent canvas suddenly flopped.

The owner dodged it, and the spreading singed hole with the flames eating it wider. He made for the other tall pole, while those behind him asked to be given a spell with the axe, or shouted encouragement. Divested of his jacket, Henry started work on the second pole.

His friends were stamping and beating on the singed canvas and making some headway, except on the side where the canvas sloped upwards towards the top of the second pole. The flames on that side stayed kindled. They leapt forward with greater speed up the burning material, helped because it was almost vertical.

Henry's axe flew even faster. The smoke bothered him. He found himself making his strokes with his smarting eyes closed to keep out the smoke. Bella called out something at the top of her voice, but he felt that if he stopped for a spell he would never start again.

Calamity followed, almost at once.

Although the axe blade had not severed the second pole, the substantial weight upheld by it caused it to give way. The splintering happened in a matter of seconds. Before Henry could draw back, or properly make the attempt to shield his head, down came the upper half of the prop, with the canvas still attached to it.

The wood caught his head a glancing blow and sent him down with his senses reeling in the path of the other canvas. One moment he was in the full view of others, and the next he was out of sight. Bella screamed with horror and led a rush to try and extricate him from canvas which was burning perilously close to the place where he had gone under.

All four of them plunged forward, utterly disregarding their own danger. Ike was the one to stumble over a booted foot. He hauled on it and called out for help. The other two men joined him, and Henry was hauled out, inches at a time. He was groaning, and did not appear to be badly injured, but Bella was past taking chances.

She assumed temporary command. 'Ike, I'd like for you to go an' bring a buckboard or somesuch, an' don't delay. Might be a good thing if you got back before Henry recovered his senses. You understand me?'

'If you're figurin' on takin' him along to the local doctor's, I do, Bella. I don't know where I'll find a 'board in all this smoke an' chaos, though. Jest the same, I'll be tryin'!'

While the little man was gone, Sam and Bill between them carried Henry clear of the marquee and settled him on the grass. They found a water canteen and applied it to his lips. He came round almost at once. By then, upwards of a dozen men were stamping and flailing the canvas in an effort to put out the fire.

Henry saw this, but his eyes slewed away to Bella. He appeared to take some comfort from her close presence, but his senses slipped away again due to the crack he had sustained on his head.

Meanwhile, Ike ran thirty yards towards the east along Main Street. He called to three people before one of them could concentrate long enough to answer him. He had just learned what he wanted to know when his informant turned and looked back in the other direction.

'There's a buckboard, stranger! It's goin' the right way, too, an' the feller up on the seat is none other than the doc! How's that for luck?'

Ike called his thanks and went back over his tracks to contact the doctor and ask for his immediate aid. Aloysius Hunt, M.D., was bobbing up and down on the seat as though he was in a saddle. He saw Ike in his path and gestured with his whip for the dwarf to stand out of his way.

Little Ike complied, but only to save himself. As the buckboard went by, he grabbed for it and managed to scramble up beside the outraged sawbones.

'Now look you here, stranger! My

business is urgent, an' I don't care to have jaspers like you takin' free rides when I'm answerin' a call! I'd be obliged if you'd get off this here buckboard in the same way as you got on'

Ike gritted his teeth. 'If you ain't the most ornery sawbones it's ever been my misfortune to come across! I'll leave this conveyance when we get to the scene of the trouble! In case you were thinkin' of goin' elsewhere, I'd like for to tell you you're now on your way to the circus site, an' the first feller you'll be dealin' with is the proprietor himself, Henry Walton!

'So save your breath, an' use it later! I hope a puff or two of smoke won't bother you, or a lick of flame, 'cause the folks tell me you're the only medical man for miles around!'

Hunt contained himself with difficulty. He managed to take one or two long sideways glances at Ike before the turning was reached to get on to the circus site. In spite of himself, the medical man was intrigued by Ike's size. His clinical observation, however, did not dissuade Ike from a spot of quizzical staring, himself.

Doctor Hunt was a good man for his age, which was sixty-six. He was spritely and fit. His hair was silver-grey. He still had plenty of it under the silk top hat which he wore for his calls. His chin beard and brows were of the same texture. His grey suit was fairly new, and of an expensive cut. In recent years he had taken to wearing pince-nez, but he missed nothing of any consequence.

During his long and varied life, he had been married twice. His two spouses were vastly different creatures, but each of them had quickly learned the secret for silencing him when he sought to use his somewhat embittered tongue upon them. Now he was a widower again.

As the watching crowd surged around the buckboard, Hunt was thinking rather maliciously that his passenger's four-and-a-half feet made his own five-and-a-half seem like the stature of a giant.

A man shouted: 'Plenty of work for you around here, Doc!'

The deep-set eyes behind the pince-nez were watchful. They took in the scene and scanned the faces of the men who had been involved in the firefighting. One or two had had their faces singed, and sustained burns on their arms and shoulders, but no one looked to need immediate attention.

'Turn the hoss around that a-way,' Ike instructed.

Hunt glanced away past the flattened and smoking marquee. Again, he could see nothing to make him think his presence was urgently required. His horse was slowing almost to a standstill when Bella loomed up right ahead of him.

Her friends had found her a pair of denims to go over the lower part of her balancing costume, and a biggish check shirt to wear above it. These borrowed clothes did nothing to enhance her beauty; rather they did the opposite.

The doctor, whose haughtiness was partly assumed through his lack of confidence with women, tried to get Bella out of the way. She declined to move. Instead, she grabbed the horse by the head and showed that she intended to keep it in check.

'I don't know who you are, miss, but you've no right to be actin' the way you are! I'm answerin' a general call to assist the men who've sustained burns here in tryin' to help the circus outfit!'

Bella delayed her reply long enough for her forthright green eyes to impale the doctor's. She saw him flinch.

'The burns these — these men have sustained are only superficial. The only man who's taken any serious risks is the owner of the circus, Henry Walton. He's been felled and rendered unconscious by a pole in the big top. *He's* the one who really needs you, an' you ought to be directin' this crowbait around there with the minimum of delay!'

Hunt was impressed by Bella's poise and her way of speaking, but he did not allow her advice to cloud his judgement.

'There's too much noise, too much smoke an' such to take this hoss over there. You'll have to think of somethin' else, miss!'

Bella made another brief survey of the position, and reluctantly agreed. 'Maybe you're right. So we'll wait here, an' Henry can be brought to meet you. In case I haven't made myself clear, he wants removin' from here to your surgery jest as soon as you can get him there!'

The doctor nodded, and then attempted to ignore her. It was not easy, however, and the sawbones found himself watching the dwarf going off with strict instructions to have the injured man brought to the conveyance. Three men hovered somewhere ahead of the shaft horse. They had dropped out of the bucket line at the first opportunity to have their burns and scratches dressed.

Bella turned on them with venom in

her eyes. 'You'd take up a doctor's time at a scene like this with *those* scratches?' she cried. 'If you haven't expired, get yourselves along to the surgery in a half-hour's time!'

Hunt held up his hand, the beginning of a protest, but Juarez and Bill Trask appeared, carrying Henry between them, and the sight of the limp body effectively stemmed his growing ire. Bella waved away the men who did not know whether to take her words seriously. Hunt became involved in draping Henry over the bed of his buckboard. As soon as the fallen man was reasonably comfortable, Bill Trask backed the shaft horse towards the street, and that was the end of the sawbones' visit to the scene of the fire.

Hunt began to nod impatiently when the board was turned around, but Trask would not let go the horse's head until Bella was seated beside the doctor and quite ready for them to move off. The girl nodded, and called for the horse to be on its way.

'I don't honestly see the purpose — ' Hunt began, reasonably enough.

'I'm comin' along with you, Doc, jest the same. You'll need a nurse, maybe, an' besides I've got a couple of sore places myself. I fell off the high wire before the fire started.'

The doctor sighed. He swallowed hard, and accepted the circumstances as they were. Ten minutes later, just as they were slowing down in front of the doctor's two-storey board residence, a horse came clattering after them and was yanked to a walk behind them.

Town Marshal Lon Farrow looked thoroughly out of sorts with himself. At forty-seven, he had sparse dark hair and grey sideburns. His brown eyes were troubled, and as he had no eyebrows his discomfiture was plainly obvious. His red face and cream-coloured Texas-style hat were begrimed. He flapped his black vest to cool his body, and cleared his throat.

'Doc, I thought to have a talk with Walton, the circus boss, but I hear he's still unconscious. Is that right?'

The lawman slipped a boot out of a stirrup and swung to the ground, moving over to the buckboard with his rather curious shambling walk.

'Never mind, Marshal, you can make yourself useful! You can help me carry him inside.'

Farrow snorted, but in the presence of the girl he refrained from making any salty comments. Between the three of them, they carried Henry's far-from-lightweight body into the surgery on the left front side of the building. Within a couple of minutes, Hunt had given his full attention to the patient. Bella came back from his kitchen with a kettle of water, which had been boiling on the stove.

Warm compresses on the skull contusion soon had Henry stirring and gaping around once more. He groaned. 'Can't remember another day when I had my eyes shut so often in daylight. Maybe it comes from tryin' to steer a big pole with my head.'

'Hm, no signs of loss of memory,' Hunt remarked, as he continued the treatment.

'Say, it sure was good of you to treat me in this fashion,' Henry ventured.

Hunt made an ominous sound, and Bella gave her boss a sharp glance, warning him not to sustain the topic. The doctor let it pass, and presently, when he was bandaging the bruised head, he permitted Henry to converse briefly with the lawman.

'Are you here to talk about the damage, or seek the cause?' Henry asked.

'Why — er — to seek the cause, I guess,' the Marshal replied.

The lawman shuffled about the room on legs which had been broken early in his adult life. He was far from being at ease. Henry surveyed him afresh while Bella and the doctor pushed the wheeled couch against the rear wall. Still reclining, and with a hand tucked behind his bandaged head, Henry began to talk.

'Somebody has been handin' out easy money again. Yesterday's escape of the big cat was due to the work of a fellow named Den Rollins. I forced a confession out of him. It's my opinion the same fellow paid Rollins, or men like him, to tamper with certain gear in my marquee, and to fire Miss Lester's wagon. These are both acts to be regretted. If you are really keen on findin' the culprits, all you have to do is to look for loafers with extra money to spend. *Comprende?*'

Farrow's red face was reddening even more, as Henry told him his business; even so, the lawman knew it was good advice. He hovered towards the surgery door.

'Don't bother your head about the circus,' Henry called after him. 'I'll see to things in a little while.'

He groaned, at the prospect of winding everything up rather than from pain. After assuring himself that Bella was staying, he turned his face to the wall and enjoined the doctor to patch her up well. The girl fought down her mild embarrassment when she had to show the sawbones the burn behind her knee. He was gentle with her, and more than a little curious about her part in the circus.

She told him a few details while he changed her dressings, and would have said more, but their ears were assailed quite suddenly by a man's sneeze. Hunt's pincenez popped off his nose and hung by their ribbon against his clinical apron.

He said, 'Hell an' tarnation!' And then: 'Pardon me, miss. I wasn't thinkin' of your presence. When we came in it never occurred to me that there might be anyone waitin' in the waitin'-room. I reckon I'd best go an' see who it is. Are you sure that hand bandage is comfortable, now?'

Bella answered him pleasantly enough, and reminded him that she had offered to act as his nurse when the burned helpers came along from the fire.

'I'll be glad to start helpin' right now,

if you like,' she suggested.

'Sure would help if you could make coffee for us, Miss Lester,' he replied, with a nod.

She went to the kitchen while he investigated the sneeze.

7

Henry remained on his couch in a semi-somnolent state.

Bella made the coffee and brought a cup for the three of them. The uncouth-looking man sitting in the wooden armchair sniffed it, but was not offered a drink. Hunt drank deep, and regarded the man from the waiting-room through and over his spectacles. Bella came to the conclusion that he did not much like what he saw. She felt she had to agree with him.

'All right, move that chair over to the table, an' take off the bandanna,' Hunt instructed.

While the newcomer busied himself in removing the soiled cloth from his right arm, Bella continued to peruse him. He was a man in his middle thirties, with greasy, neutral-coloured hair. His bulky body and soiled clothing had an unwashed aroma about them. The swarthy skin was a stranger to soap, and the frown on the ill-assorted features looked as if it stayed there twenty-four hours a day.

Hunt studied the wound and breathed out rather heavily.

'Hm, quite a nasty scratch. Deep, too. You say it was done by a cat?'

'Sure, one of the worst kind of cats — tigers! The ones down at the circus. I don't figure you were down there when they started squallin' to be let out, but they came through the crowd like they was runnin' for their lives when the doors were opened! I ain't never seen anythin' like it!'

Hunt glanced across at Bella, and then to where Henry was lying with his face averted by the wall.

'You must have been a little slow gettin' out of the way,' he opined.

The patient nodded several times, while a fresh bowl of hot water was poured out and laced with antiseptic. Henry quietly cleared his throat, but the patient talked on.

'I sure was. One moment we were all surgin' forward, an' the next there was this huge cat comin' right at me! I threw up my arm to protect my face an' this was what I got for my trouble!'

The doctor went to work with the bathing. Bella, unbidden, murmured: 'You must have been very unfortunate, mister. Still, you got away from the scene of the accident without wastin' much time. I didn't see you after you'd been scratched, nor did I talk with anybody who knew about it.'

The patient, Heath, winced as the stinging fluid touched his wound. He realised that there was something special behind Bella's remarks, and he protested.

'What do I mean?' the girl repeated thoughtfully. 'Well, funny things have been happenin' at the circus. The big cat's cage was opened by somebody who didn't wait to be told. Before that, maybe the same someone fired my wagon, an' then there's the matter of the high wire that wasn't safe!'

Hunt was surprised by the depth of feeling in Bella's voice.

'Miss Lester, you surprise me a little. Do you have any reason to suspect this man had anythin' to do with the circus's setbacks?'

Bella glanced across at Henry, whose eyes were open. He nodded to her, thinking that what she was going to try might be worth while.

'I know about animals, Doc. The big cat didn't stop to scratch this galoot when it was fleein' for its life away from the fire! I'm sayin' the scratch most likely was put on his arm *before* the tiger got loose. In plain American, he could have been the one to unlock the door! Khan was crazy enough to scratch anyone tamperin' with the lock, even though he knew it meant freedom!'

'But — but this girl, she's crazy,' Heath protested. 'Why would I want to set the cat loose, anyways?'

'Why wouldn't you, if the money was

right?' Bella threw back at him.

Henry cleared his throat. 'Khan shot out of his cage as though he'd been burned, when he eventually came out! He didn't stop to scratch anybody. Before I could get in a tellin' shot he'd run for a wagon an' hidden himself underneath. A certain fellow of my acquaintance then shot him dead while he was still under there! I think Bella has stumbled on the truth!'

Hunt's restraining hand kept the patient in the chair. The bandage was going on now. They could see the haunted look behind his eyes. Bella's memory was active. She thought back to the encounter with Rudge on the trail.

'Did you happen to have a meetin' with a certain man on the north side of the trail, east of this town, earlier today?'

Again, the twinkle of guilt showed in Heath's eyes. Henry thumbed back the hammer of a hand gun. Suddenly, the fellow capitulated.

'You're right,' he admitted. 'You must have second sight, or somethin'. I *did* unlock that cage, but I didn't think what we were paid to do would cause the whole circus to fold up, honest I didn't!'

Henry sat up slowly. 'But that's the way it'll work out, mister. Miss Lester, here, has been injured. We've lost the big top, two wagons an' all the wild animals, so far as I know. That's a mighty serious series of happenings. Maybe it would help you if you made a clean breast of the whole thing. It sure is a pity the marshal left before you came in here.'

Heath gasped. He was beginning to see things in perspective. In admitting his guilt, he was talking himself and his partner, Alonso, into a long spell in the penitentiary. His brain began to work clearly at last.

'Leave things to me,' he suggested, as heavy feet sounded in the waiting-room. 'You'll be busy for a while with the other injured. I'll go along to the peace office an' try an' straighten things out a little with the marshal. I sure am sorry for the way things have turned out.'

Henry replaced his gun. He winced at a head pain when he lowered his legs to the ground, and decided against going out of the room for a while. The doctor shrugged, leaving the matter in the hands of the other two. Bella decided to wait for Henry's guidance. She helped him back on to the couch, talking easily to him, and wondering how many men, burned and smelling of fire, would come along for medical attention.

* * *

An hour and a half went by, during which the men with minor burns were gradually dealt with. Hunt politely asked Bella if she would care to fix a meal for the three of them. In the circumstances, she felt it hard to do otherwise. The stove was still keeping her busy when the last patient had gone and a riding horse arrived.

Marshal Farrow strolled into the surgery, removing his hat and shaking his head most decidedly. He found the doctor sitting back behind his table smoking a pipe, and Henry sitting up and feeling much better for the rest and the treatment.

'Well,' Henry remarked, 'did you get a full statement?'

Farrow slumped into the patients' chair and cleared his throat. 'All I've had since I left here is a lot of conjecture. Empty statements, I'd say, if you pressed me!'

He favoured his listeners with one of his rare, un-illuminating smiles and wondered why they were not at least more contented-looking now that he had tried. Bella came tripping into the room in a pair of borrowed slippers.

'Did I hear you to say you didn't get the statement from the jasper who let the big cat free?'

'What is all this?' Farrow protested.

He had to wait another couple of minutes before Henry explained what was in all their minds. 'A man with a bad cat scratch was in here for treatment. He as good as admitted that he had been involved with openin' the cage door an' other things. Went away from here on his own say-so, to find you an' to make a full statement of his misdeeds. Seems he went right on out an' kept on walkin'.'

'Ridin' is more likely,' Hunt added sagely.

The explanations were completed, and Farrow wanted to be on his way again to try and identify a man who fitted the description. Henry was the one to delay him.

'Take it from us, Marshal, he won't still be around town. Firin' wagons is still a mighty unpleasant form of law-breakin'. We were fools ever to let him walk out of here under his own steam. Still, it can't be helped.'

Hunt thought otherwise. He it was who gave Marshal Farrow a full description of the man with the wounded arm, and who encouraged the disconsolate lawman to make a tour of the liveries and bars once again on the offchance of apprehending the wrongdoer.

Henry yawned as the lawman left. He yawned again as Bella assisted him into the kitchen, after the doctor. He murmured, 'For my money, Bella, what's left of it, young Jerry Rudge has been pushin' too hard this last day or two. As soon as I've wound things up an' taken a little rest I'm goin' to see about him. It won't be pleasant work, runnin' him down to earth, but I feel I owe it to myself, an' everyone else who worked for the circus.'

'I feel exactly the same way myself,' the girl admitted. 'But you must give yourself a chance to recover first.'

Hunt was whistling when they reached the kitchen. They could tell by his manner that they would be invited to spend the night in his spacious house.

* * *

During the ensuing forty-eight hours, the searchings of the local peace officers produced no results. Den Rollins had left town. So had the man Heath and his riding partner, Alonso. Jerry Rudge had checked out of the hotel, and all the information Henry could glean was a vague notion as to the direction in which the young villain had gone.

The circus marquee was a write-off. So were two wagons, and the whole stock of wild animals. The last of the cats had been cornered in an alley within an hour of its release and shot without difficulty.

Henry's head cleared after one good night's sleep. He chose that first morning to make his peace with the Marshal and the town notables. The Mayor, and others, expressed their sympathy and wondered what his intentions were for the future.

Henry made it quite clear that he had no intention of trying to go on as a circus proprietor; at least, not straight away. He wanted, so he told them, to dispose of his useful stock to anyone in the area who was interested. In that way, he would be able to reimburse certain of his employees who had forgone their wages in the recent past so that he would have the capital to replace a few costly but necessary items.

He refused a loan with good grace, and accepted the offer of a large barn in which he could hold an auction of his unwanted gear.

The big sale took place at nine o'clock on the second morning, and within a short time of that hour, the place was jammed to capacity. It soon became apparent that those with money in the immediate vicinity of town were going to bid for his things, in an effort to help him wind up his affairs.

As the big items were offered, he took prospective buyers out at the rear of the barn and allowed them to examine the lots.

Altogether, he put up one big wagon, three cages and two carts. The cages had to go cheaply, but the wagon and carts fetched good prices. He was adequately recompensed for eight harness horses, and well rewarded for four of his performing horses which he sold in pairs.

The two whites went to a local rancher, and a buyer from the next town farther west paid generously for the blacks. Around eleven o'clock all the bidding and selling was completed. Those who had come to make the sale a success were thanked for their kindness, and the barn was gradually cleared.

The men who had been employed as temporary local labour were then paid, and given a small bonus for helping to fight the fire. Henry wanted to get to his accounting, and for a time his friends were a source of embarrassment to him. Eventually, he handed over several dollars to Bill Trask and asked him to buy suitable drinks for them all.

They left him to work out his money and his commitments.

A little after six in the evening, the whole party met in a curtained alcove at the back of the largest eating house in town. Henry headed the table, which was a large one, made out of three ordinary-sized ones pushed together.

A drink was brought in for everybody, and then the awaited speech was given. In a sober, matter-of-fact voice, Henry told how much he had appreciated the present company, and how circumstances, and not his wishes, now made it necessary for them to part.

'We have been a good family,' he went on, 'but the day of parting is tomorrow for us. After what has happened recently, I don't want to carry on my business. I have other things to see to, things which I would not want you to share with me, things I wouldn't want to discuss in front of children.'

Bill Trask sighed. Sam murmured a religious expression, and his wife dabbed furtively at her eyes. Bella kept her eyes averted, but her lips were never quite still. She was feeling the occasion as much as anyone. Little Ike's mouth drooped at the outer corners. Even the gay Juarez children were aware of the gravity of the moment.

Henry tried to make light of it, but he did not succeed.

'Now, as to the sale and the settling up. If any of you are worried about my finances, don't. I got a good price for everythin', an' all will be paid. You, Sam, lost your wagon with all your family's personal things in it. After today, I shan't need a wagon. I want you to take over mine, along with the two horses which we've kept. Also some two hundred dollars are due to you in lieu of back wages. No protests, please!'

'Bill will have a tidy sum to collect from me, an' he keeps his performin' mule, which I didn't have the heart to sell. Ike will keep his throwin' knives, an' anythin' else he fancies in the way of equipment. I'll have a few months' wages for him, too.'

'Bella, you lost your wagon. I'm turnin' over to you the value of the wagon I sold, as well as the price of two harness hosses. Also I want you to keep the sorrel mare for your own personal use. There'll be money, as well. I guess that about takes care of everythin' except to tell you I'll be ridin' out come tomorrow on the back of the palomino!

'If we could manage it now, I'd like for us to put a good face on things an' do justice to the meal that's bein' prepared for us!'

With an obvious effort, he pushed back his chair and called gaily for the proprietor. Knowing what each of them best liked to drink, he ordered accordingly. In time, the gathering contrived to forget that this was their last meal together as a working unit, but by the time they moved to their beds their gaiety had died again.

Henry, himself, passed a restless night, hovering between sleep and wakefulness.

8

All regular members of the circus outfit rose early the following morning. The Juarez family were still on the camp site, and the others had made use of rooms in the biggest hotel. Men and women alike were unsettled by the coming split in the working unit. The Mexicans were decided as to what they would do. As soon as the early morning chores were over they were heading for the Mexican border to seek a decent living in the country of their birth.

Bella, Little Ike and Bill Trask were still very much undecided. Indecision showed in their faces when they made their way across to the open ground to give the Mexican family a send-off.

Henry was there before them. Although his regard for the others was known to be warm, he was strangely bashful, as though he was meeting distant relations after a long separation. Sam Juarez made a little speech, backed up and prompted by his buxom wife, Juanita. The parting dragged a little.

Bill and Ike started the actual break by moving around the wagon to check over the traces. Eventually, Sam ran out of breath and began to look depressed. He cracked his whip and stood up on the box, calling out his farewells and wishes for future good luck and happiness.

Henry backed away to the edge of the open space, waving until the wagon had jingled out of sight. He sighed, stuck his hands on his hips, and glanced from one to another of the three people who were still with him.

'Have you folks had breakfast yet?' he queried.

'No, we haven't,' Bella informed him, 'and the same goes for you! Is there any reason why we can't eat a mornin' meal together an' have a last talk?'

'None at all, I guess,' Henry admitted.

The townsfolk had decided that the circus outfit was jinxed, and every time a local man or woman came near the performers there was a tendency to quieten the conversation and stare. Henry hated this atmosphere more than any of the others. He wanted to be out of it, on his way.

'Why don't we go over to the eatin' house right now, an' order up a good meal, then?' Bill suggested brusquely.

'Why don't you three do that?' Henry countered. 'Me, I've got to make a short call on the doctor before he starts out on his rounds. You can order for four, though, because I shan't be long.'

Little Ike was about to try and stop him going off altogether when Bella made a gesture which dissuaded him.

She said, 'All right, Henry, we'll be waitin' for you. Don't let the food go cold. An' give our warm regards to the doctor.'

* * *

Henry was away twenty minutes, but his food was kept hot for him. He ate with a good appetite, while his friends thought of the last things they wanted to say to him.

'Are you certain sure you want us to leave you, Henry, right after this meal?' Bill wanted to know.

'Absolutely certain, Bill. It ain't that I've taken a dislike to your company. I'll never forget the way you worked for the circus, or how you behaved durin' the fire. It's — well — it's this jinx business. The locals talk about a jinx. Well, you an' I know the jinx is a real person, an' things have gone so far between him an' me that I have to do somethin' about it. The trouble started long before we met up to work together, an' he sure has a lot to answer for, believe me! If I wanted help, I'd sure enough tell you now, but it ain't that way, not that way at all! I surely hope you'll understand!'

He glanced around the faces of the others as though they might be a long way from understanding him. Ike and

Bill looked sober and resigned to the state of affairs as Henry had outlined them. Bella still had things to say.

'While you were along there at the doctor's, the three of us did some talkin'. Ike an' Bill, here, think they might have some difficulty in gettin' jobs to suit them. I'm restless, too. For a time, though, the three of us have decided to stick together. We want you to know that if our trails cross in the future you can still depend on us for help and friendship. An' that, I think, is about all you've left for us to say.'

Bella's wide-set eyes were swimming with unbidden tears. With a catch in her throat, she lowered her head. Henry laid a gentle hand on her shoulder, and promptly lost all interest in the rest of his food. He glanced at the two men. His eyes begged them to say something to tide him over this moment of deep emotion.

Ike was at a loss, and Bill had to scratch his skull several times before the obvious occurred to him.

'Will you — can you tell us which direction you're likely to be headin' in? Or is it a secret?'

Bella stifled a sob and looked up into Henry's face.

'I don't know a whole lot about the future, myself. All I can say is it looks as if I'll travel south-east for a day or two.' He stood up, feeling the situation very acutely, and determined to pay the bill and be off. He had paid present company and others the night before. All he owed was a small amount to the livery. 'You don't need to rush your food on my account,' he added.

Bella rose at the same time. She confronted him, reached up and put her arms round his neck. She kissed him, in full view of their friends, and felt the warmth surge out of him as he co-operated.

'I want you to know that I understand, an' — an' that I'm sorry we weren't closer to one another before the fire came along an' spoiled everythin'. I ought to have known you never did that shameful thing back in Stillwater! Shame on me for doubtin' you!'

Henry kissed her again, and murmured his thanks for her sympathetic parting words into her ear. Then he put her from him, and hastily shook hands with the men as the proprietor came in to say that a livery hand had brought along the palomino. His roll had been collected from the hotel, as well. All he had to do was swing his leg into the saddle and ride.

The puzzled livery hand thought he made hard work of it, as he fingered the payment for his boss and watched the send-off party with their strained faces. He wondered where he had seen such an assembly before. Presently, his mind clicked. He was seeing expressions such as mourners wore on Boot Hill.

⋆ ⋆ ⋆

Four days later, Henry was still steadfastly riding in the same direction;

namely, towards the south-east. He had briefly called at two small towns which were little more than a broadening in the trail. A dollar here and there had loosened tongues sufficiently to make him believe that Jerry Rudge was on ahead of him. He did not need much encouragement to keep on riding in the young villain's wake.

What exactly he would do when Rudge was overtaken, he was not quite sure. Perhaps it would all end in a gun showdown. Certainly, the fellow would never do any good in adult life. All he would do would be to cause trouble for innocent folks whose lives happened to become twisted with his.

Henry refrained as much as possible from thinking about the outcome. Hard riding had helped him to take his mind off the circus which had been his bread and butter, indeed his very existence for so long. In losing his outfit he seemed to have achieved a better understanding with Bella. The knowledge of that had warmed him, but he could hardly have brought her along with him on a vengeance trail against a man with whom she had been brought up.

He was cogitating over these matters at eleven in the morning when the patient palomino twitched its ears, indicating the presence of something, or someone, this far undetected by its master.

Five minutes later, a poorly-marked private diverging trail on the north side of the track drew Henry to a squat little shack with evidence round about it of steady human toil. At the side of the building, a gaunt elderly man with a slight stoop was sucking at a clay pipe and scratching his belly through a soiled shirt. His hair was grey, tousled and thin.

Henry said, 'Howdy. Are you contemplatin' the weather, or plannin' on a spell of work?'

The homesteader, a loner, shifted the pipe around the side of his mouth and viewed the horse and rider from shrewd eroded eyes. He stamped his boots on a pebbled path, drawing Henry's attention to his bandiness and the leather leggings into which his denims were tucked.

He nodded. 'Could be the answer to that question depended on whether you want work or not.'

Henry dismounted and grinned easily. 'I'm not lookin' for regular work, old timer. I'm more interested in information at the present time. But if there's somethin' that won't take too long where I can help, then I won't refuse.'

'Clancy McCord never turned a fellow away without a drink of coffee to slake his thirst. Come on in.'

Henry cleaned up in the one-roomed home, and drank the proffered coffee. He was surprised to see the place kept so tidy.

'I've been waitin' for a fellow with energy in his body to help me hoist some heavy sacks on to my wagon. If you'll help, I can get on my way to the miller in town. Think you could hold back for half an hour to help? Could be I'd have the information you're wantin' if you have the patience!'

'I'm askin' after a man who rode the same trail ahead of me,' Henry explained, as he tried to hide his eagerness.

'Not many men go through this way unnoticed by me,' McCord assured him.

Ten minutes later, they were bringing sacks out of a shed at the back and stacking them on the boards of a stout cart. Henry shooed the homesteader away to harness his two horses, and finished the lifting and carrying himself. The few verbal exchanges which passed between them as the work was going on made Henry believe that McCord might be a useful source of information. Almost exactly half an hour later the cart was loaded and the horses were in the shafts.

Henry made good use of some pump water and gave the palomino a brief grooming. To his surprise, McCord clambered up on the box of the cart and showed every intention of leaving promptly.

'Hey, old timer, haven't you forgotten somethin'?'

Clancy grinned. His pipe swung a little in a gap between two ancient teeth. 'You mean about the information? That won't hold us back. I can give you that on the way into Junction.'

'You won't be takin' me out of my way, in the event I have to act on the information?'

Having been assured on that point, the rider mounted up again and patiently walked his mount alongside the cart. He was prompted to describe the man whom he was seeking, and as he struggled to put Jerry Rudge into words, McCord punctuated his efforts with nods.

'All right,' he said at last, 'I figure I've heard enough. There was a feller through a day or two ago. Went on into Junction, then came out again, so I've heard. Had a feelin' for solitude. Might have been hard up for money, or tryin' to hide himself. I ain't good on talkin' descriptions, but I'd say he fitted the talk you've jest made.'

'An' where is he now?' Henry prompted.

'I figure you'll need to look at the old Parson Brook shack. Can't say whether he'll still be there, though, 'cause nobody goes near the shack these days. You see, the old parson got the idea the Almighty didn't like the way he was ministerin' to his flock, so he up with his gun an' shot himself!'

Henry was intrigued by the story of the parson's end, and even more fascinated by the prospect of overtaking Rudge. Still some little distance short of town, McCord directed him off-trail on the north side, and told him to look for a little wooden place at the foot of a slope, watered by a shallow stream.

Thirty minutes was sufficient time to bring the dwelling into view. It had a crescent of timber at the rear, and the stream wound across the front of it about fifty yards short of the building. The grass was high on the small diamond-shaped swale. There was no sign of humans.

Henry pulled up a furlong short, sitting the palomino, which drank a few mouthfuls of water out of the trickling stream beside them. Rudge was known to be a treacherous man, but he could hardly have used an old-timer like Clancy McCord to set up a trap for an enemy in this remote spot.

On the lower ground, the stream had once etched out for itself a gully. Only a harebrained fool would have declined to use the shelter it gave in approaching a doubtful spot. Henry dismounted, pulled his Winchester out of the scabbard, and availed himself of plenty of spare ammunition. He figured that McCord would have chuckled if he could have seen him making such elaborate preparations for the meeting.

He left the palomino behind, with the saddle slackened, and kept his descent quiet as the swale and the cabin came nearer. In his approach he startled a jay, and a hare leapt distractingly through the long grass, but no human showed himself, and there were no indications whatever that the shack was, or had been recently, occupied. After resting in the arroyo for upwards of five minutes at the nearest spot to the dwelling, Henry raised himself and crawled forward through the long grass. A close observer could have seen the grass moving, but until the newcomer had to get over the corral-type fence he would have remained a mystery to anyone in the vicinity.

He ran the rest of the way, and was pleased when the door gave under his touch. Only the squeak of unoiled hinges heralded his entry. There were cobwebs and dust everywhere, but it had been visited in the recent past. Someone had wiped the dust off the rickety table and left a slip of paper there.

Henry crossed to the table, making no sound on the beaten earth floor. He glanced down at the paper, and the purport of the text made him put his face nearer.

It said: *If you get this far, I wish you luck, because you're going to need it. J.R.*

There was only one J.R. in the world for Henry. The message was a warning, and it probably meant that Rudge was setting something up for him in the immediate future. Where more likely than in a forgotten shack where a poor parson had taken his own life?

The jingle of a spur wheel came almost at once. It was somewhere out at the back. He moved to a window which almost defied his effort to look out, owing to its griminess. Behind the tree crescent were two, possibly three, riding horses, on lower ground. The first rifle shot made him drop to earth. It was as well he was prepared. The bullet holed the pane through which he had been looking, and at the same time made him wonder about his chances of slipping out again and getting back up the gully.

He moved hurriedly back, staying on his knees, and started to push the door closed with his rifle barrel. He had moved it a foot when a bullet, fired at an angle from somewhere out at the front, chipped splinters of wood out of it, making him duck. From wide on the other extreme, possibly from the arroyo itself, another bullet winged through the lessening gap and found a way out through another glass pane.

Henry slammed the door, and put the bar across it, being thankful over that. Flying lead came at him from three angles. He became aware that the marksmen were closing in. Every now and again, he fired back, but the glimpses he saw of his opponents were only brief ones, usually accompanied by a telling gun flash. He knew that he was only delaying them, and that without help he would, presumably, be doomed by nightfall.

Although his fate appeared to be sealed, he was slow to let depression get him down. He took the opportunity, during the middle hours of the day, of looking back on his recent actions. A bystander, assessing the situation into which he had placed himself, would have said he had dismissed his friends at the worst time possible.

Around one o'clock, a bullet, better sighted than most, came out of the tree stand and ventilated his hat.

9

Bella, Bill and Little Ike approached the place where Henry had left the trail to look for the parson's cabin about two hours after the off-trail siege had begun. Distant echoes carried to them and made them think the same kind of thoughts.

Since the parting with Henry in Chaparral, they had been following him. Bella professed to have no particular destination of her own, and the other two had gone along with her for company and to give her protection in the event that she should ever want it. They knew that she had once lived in Stillwater, San Juanito County, New Mexico, and they surmised that if they didn't run into complications through being tied in with Henry's vengeance trail that she would lead them all the way back to the place where she was raised.

The gunfire halted them rather abruptly. During the previous twenty-four hours they had speeded up their progress with the idea of overtaking Henry and persuading him, against his earlier inclinations, to take them along with him. Bella had curtailed the midday halt to a mere half-hour because of her yearnings for the sight of him.

She felt sudden fear on his behalf as Bill dismounted and examined the horse's shoe prints leading off the trail. Ike also dismounted, and took charge of the reins of all three. Bill was slow to make up his mind.

'Well, I wouldn't swear to it,' he murmured at last. 'There's this single hoss been sidin' a cart since that place a mile or two back. I've seen so much of this one hoss's track since we left Chaparral, I'd gamble this sign belonged to the palomino!'

'At worst, that could mean Henry's hit trouble,' Bella surmised.

'It certainly looks that way, but we could be wrong, of course,' Ike remarked, without conviction.

'But we've come a long way, an' always in the back of our minds has been Henry an' the trouble he could meet with!' Bella added.

During this brief altercation, Bill had been straining his ears. Without giving any explanation, he trotted off down the side track, favouring his weaker leg. Ike muttered that Bill was on to something they had overlooked. He started to fish around in his saddle pockets and brought out some of the throwing knives which he had used in his act. Bella matched his reactions by taking from her saddle pocket a gunbelt with two holsters. She fitted a .45 Colt into one of them, and waited, feeling rather uncertain of herself.

A minute later, Bill, who had gone out of sight, called out to them. Ike scampered after him and whistled in surprise when he saw the older man coming back leading the palomino by the reins. A sharp pair of rifle cracks echoed and re-echoed as the trio stood close, making up their minds about the latest development.

'We've got to assume he's in trouble,' Bella muttered. 'Otherwise he might have to struggle with more trouble than he can handle, an' not be any better off with us so close.'

'This is man's work,' the dwarf opined in his high-pitched voice.

Bill remarked: 'I'm wonderin' how Bella can help while we two go down there an' investigate.' Suddenly he brightened. 'Why don't you ride on into town an' get help? You can tell them what's goin' on! They'll remember that one-night show we did for them not so long ago!'

The girl appreciated the point. She mopped her brow and reseated the cream-coloured flat-crowned hat which she had been using of late.

'But I'm a good shot with hand guns,' she argued. 'You both know that! Why shouldn't *I* go down there with you? Nobody would expect a girl to shoot like *I* can!'

Bill looked up into her face. 'Right now, it sure does sound like a shoulder-gun battle. It could stay that way. Besides, I don't think Henry would like it if he knew you were killin' for his sake, Bella. I think he looks upon you as kind of special!'

The girl caught her breath and blushed. 'You really think that, Bill?'

'We both do,' Ike cut in. 'An' what's more, we've held this opinion for quite a time.'

'All right, then,' the girl conceded. 'I'll ride on into town an' do what I can about bringin' help out here! As like as not I'd better start movin' right away. I wouldn't want to hold you back, on account of bullets do their dirty work in a swift fashion!'

Bill stepped aside, said something to give her confidence, and immediately mounted up again, taking the palomino in tow. One behind the other, the ex-rodeo rider and the dwarf urged their cayuses towards the scene of the action. Little Ike called forward to his partner as a sudden snag occurred to him.

'Hey, Bill, what about the mule? Ain't he goin' to get himself lost, now we've turned off-trail? Last time I caught a glimpse of him he was half a mile behind. I don't figure he ought to be allowed to make his own way. It's a sure way to lose him for good!'

'Don't you go worryin' your head none about the mule! He'll be along jest as soon as he's ready. His nose is as good as that of any hoss, too! An' you know what happens to anybody he don't fancy who tries to clap a saddle on him.'

That topic faded. The resolute pair left the three horses at a higher level than Henry had done, being forewarned. They fanned out, short of the swale, assuming correctly that Henry was holed up in the cabin. Their approach work was slow and careful. Ike's lack of stature was an advantage in this type of action. Only the heavy weapons impeded him, along with the heat of the sun.

The dwarf followed the same route that Henry had taken earlier. There was no one in the arroyo to deny him access to the meadow or the shack, but one of the attackers had climbed out of the gully not long before. Ike's caution showed him in a short space of time that he was directly behind a man making his way closer.

The gunman ahead of Ike fired one rifle shot from the long grass in front of the shack, and then he went quiet. While his two partners kept up a fairly steady fire from the rear and north sides of the shack, the man in front kept crawling forward. He, so it seemed, was the one who would eventually rush the lone defender.

Ike thought about him quite a lot. He was still thinking when Bill started to use his gun wide of the man on the north side. The first use of that weapon made a great deal of difference. The man in the long grass sank lower and awaited developments. Henry had more to think about. He was now aware of another weapon, not necessarily directed against himself.

The man whose hat brim had been singed perhaps thought more and felt more about this unexpected development. He laid low for three or four minutes, and then started to work his way back in the direction from which he had come; that is to say, towards the rear. Bill fired again and again, and made his progress slow and difficult.

Ike had still not betrayed his presence. He had rightly decided that the fellow up ahead of him would have to be eliminated before they had the initiative. His patience was rewarded. When the fellow attempted to glide over the fence masked by the grass, the dwarf saw his chance. He had a throwing knife already in his hand. Bravado, rather than a sense of fair play, made him call out just before he released the weapon.

The surprised attacker slowed up and turned. As a result, the knife which would have pierced his back entered his body through the chest. He sagged against the fence, his booted feet going away from him. His breath escaped his lips in a ragged sigh. The blade had done its work well.

Ike was about to shout to Henry about the change. Before the cry had left his lips, however, a piercing whistle out on the other flank gave warning of another development. The big lop-eared performing mule had followed its master down the lesser track. The whistle had summoned him to the exact place where Bill was hunkered down.

Sheltered by a tree bole, Trask rose to his feet and stroked the mule's head. He pointed it in the direction of the man he was shooting at, and encouraged it to go after him. The animal snorted a couple of times, but Bill had his way. It galloped off down a line just wide of the shortest distance between the antagonists.

The attacker saw it, of course, but before he could shorten its life with a well-aimed shell or two, Bill was firing his rifle as fast as he could lever and aim. The man who opposed them was in a quandary. He was slow to adjust to new developments. He had a big-boned skull, a lantern jaw, and close-set eyes which he blinked frequently, seemingly in bewilderment.

Common sense reminded him to keep well down until his opponent's rifle was empty. This he contrived to do without mishap. He then decided to use his weapon first on the mule, which had halved the distance between them. Its elusiveness was something he knew nothing about, however, and when he started to put bullets near it, it danced and leapt first one way and then the other.

His nearest bullet was no nearer to it than three inches. Baffled by the trained animal's sagacity, he gradually emptied his own weapon to no avail. On went the mule, and the time was slipping by. Any time soon, the rifleman would have him in his sights again. Suddenly the fellow panicked.

He broke cover and went away at a crouching run, always harassed by the quadruped which came steadily nearer. On a couple of occasions the animal's jinxing run prevented a killing, as the runaway was screened. Rather than risk his mule a serious injury from a hand gun, Bill whistled it back.

Henry tried to knock over the escaper with three well-placed bullets. He failed, though his shots went perilously close. After that, he put down his hot Winchester and waited for his friends to make their way to the hut. Two of the attackers pulled out on horseback, and that ended the affair.

Ike got into the cabin ahead of Bill, and Henry had him in a bear hug of delight and relief by the time Bill moved in, breathing hard.

When the greetings were over, Bill asked: 'Well, Henry, was it the fellow you were tailin', Jerry Rudge?'

'I don't reckon he was in on the shootin', but I'm sure he set up the ambush, though. You see, Rudge was supposed to be holed up here. These three guns simply waited until I moved in an' then started shootin'.'

Henry became aware of Ike cleaning one of his knives. The conversation faded, and all three went out to inspect the mortal remains of the dead enemy.

* * *

Kit Kelly, Town Marshal of Junction, also inspected the body exactly one hour later. He was a devotee of circuses and a keen admirer of Bella. She had had no difficulty in getting him to come along with her to the scene of the action, although he declined to deputise special riders and only brought with him a regular deputy, Bummer Gates.

Kelly was a brown-moustached, barrel-chested, bald-headed man in his late forties. He had a ruddy face and a tall dun stetson, dented at the front. He liked it when the going was easy, but when anyone disturbed the peace he turned mean, and was a formidable character to clash with.

Deputy Gates was nearly twenty years his junior; a short, squat man with a round black hat, and a reputation for being almost speechless.

Together, they studied the features of the dead man. In life, he had been tall, lean and muscular. His head was covered with tight, close, fair curls. His cheeks were hollowed, and his brown eyes were bulbous and heavy-lidded. He had died with his eyes open and also his mouth. Somewhere along the line his upper and lower front teeth had been badly chipped.

'Well,' Kelly began, 'we can't pretend we don't know his face, although he ain't been around town for more than a week or two. Do you have any idea of his name, Bummer?'

Deputy Gates shot a quick glance at the three strange male listeners, and then at Bella, who was near the shack door.

'Coffee's ready, boys!'

There was joy and relief in Bella's

voice, and none noticed it more than Henry. But he was desperately keen to hear what the deputy knew about the dead man. He waved to the girl, and at once turned his attention to the deputy again.

Gates murmured: 'I think he's called Kent, or some-such name as that. He . . .'

'He what?' Kelly prompted brusquely.

'He's known to Long Tom Brett an' Big Maria. Couldn't say if he's been stayin' with them, though.'

'I think that's all we need to know, for now,' Kelly decided, straightening his back. 'Let's go take the coffee now, then we'll be gettin' back into town.'

He explained as they were drinking that Long Tom Brett and Big Maria kept a rooming house. At one time they had moved about a lot, and been far less respectable than they were now. He figured that a little pressure correctly applied would yield some useful information from the couple.

* * *

As soon as the party reached Junction, Henry was resilient again and ready to take up the search for Rudge, but Kelly — on his own territory — was formidable. The Marshal ushered the whole party into an eating house on the near side of town. He acted almost as though he was conducting them to his cell block.

'I'll be back for you shortly,' he promised Henry. 'Got to talk to Long Tom myself, first.'

Henry approved this course of action, and found it easy to talk with Bella about incidents which had happened to them since they parted company. He made it quite clear that he was pleased they had followed him, and that he owed his deliverance to their continued concern about his welfare.

Bella took this to mean that he would now be glad to have them along with him, and consequently she talked easily of this and that, and secretly hoped that the earth would have swallowed up Jerry Rudge and put an end to the whole unsavoury business.

* * *

Kelly interviewed Long Tom in the rooming-house kitchen while Big Maria was giving the paying guests their evening meal in the next room. She fussed and fluttered in and out, rustling her drapes and rolling her eyes, and secretly imploring Tom not to go against the Marshal in the slightest detail.

Kelly toyed with his hat, and from time to time stroked his bald pate. 'No doubt at all about the fellow's identity,' he went on, in a hushed but very definite tone. 'My deputy identified him as Kent, Dick Kent. Now, we know you are acquainted with him, Tom, an' if you want to stay in this town an' live the quiet, respectable life, you'll tell me what I want to know without bein' difficult!'

Maria passed by with two bowls of

hot food. She whispered: 'Tell him, Tom! Don't let him move us on!'

The tall man looked suddenly older. He crossed to a mirror, glanced at his reflection in it, and then sat down. Long Tom was thirty-seven. His black hair was parted down the middle. He had a cleft chin, the left side of which showed a burn scar, and hinted at his earlier life. He turned up his shirt sleeves another two inches, donned the jacket of his dark suit, and wrinkled his forehead.

'All right, what did you want to know, Marshal?'

'The other two men who were with Kent. Are they back here, or holed up somewhere else in town?'

Tom shook his head. 'No, they rode out an' they haven't come back. I guess they'll keep right on goin' if they've clashed with you. They have that much sense.'

Kelly received the information poker-faced. 'Who was it paid them to ambush a man today?'

'I don't know, but I have my suspicions,' Tom confessed. 'A man at the big hotel. I could take you to him.'

Kelly blinked his eyes several times, then nodded. 'You stay right here, Tom. I'm goin' to contact the man who was ambushed. This man's name is Walton. He used to be a circus proprietor until quite recently.'

Tom nodded and went back to helping Maria with the evening meal.

Henry Walton knocked on the door twenty minutes later. Most lawmen would have insisted on going along to a confrontation of this kind, but Kelly figured that Walton had suffered enough to be allowed a head start. So Henry made himself known to Long Tom, and the pair of them left together, bound for the town's main hotel, which gave a superior service to Tom's rooming house.

As they walked the boards, Tom flexed and unflexed the fingers of his big hands. He had a single gun strapped to his waist, and he glanced down at

Henry's Colt. The latter noticed his interest.

'Mister, you don't have to worry none about this comin' interview. It's my risk, an' I don't aim to have you share it with me. Takin' me along to the fellow's room is enough. I'll go first an' make the challenge.'

Tom was pleased and impressed. 'As you wish, Mister Walton, only — well — I haven't always been a harmless rooming-house keeper.'

Henry chuckled and patted him on the shoulder. 'We'll go together, only I'll lead when we head for the room.'

Tom had nothing further to say. From time to time he touched his straw hat and smiled at strollers who knew him. Otherwise, he seemed to have withdrawn into himself. They reached the foyer of the hotel without incident and slowed up, by common unspoken consent. Tom nodded towards the carpeted staircase. Henry glanced all around the vestibule, but found it deserted. It bothered him that his neck hairs prickled this far from the room.

There were ten stairs in the first flight, then a ninety-degree turn, and another ten, leading to the upper corridors. Solemnly, and in step, they strode up to the turn, made it, and continued to the upper floor. With four steps to go, Henry decided to dart ahead, in case Tom had any secret thoughts about heroics. Even as he bent at the hips and sprang ahead, so a curtain moved in the entrance below and behind them, and a six-gun briefly lanced flame.

The bullet meant for Henry missed him and hit Long Tom, who had been screened on the far side of him until the sudden move. Tom staggered; Henry groaned and cried out in alarm. He hauled out his .45 and blasted off at the figure which left the screening curtain and ducked below the stairs for the receptionist's counter.

Three bullets punctuated the killer's hurried progress. Tom's slumping figure fell against Henry, who paused on the point of running back down the stairs. Already the tall man's eyes were glazing over. He summoned up his waning strength and murmured: 'Third — third door on the left.'

Henry lowered him to the carpet, thanked him as he expired, and retraced his steps. As he danced out of the rear door, two bullets made him pull up short. The other fellow was moving fast, but Henry felt he recognised the shape of the figure and the way it moved.

He went after it, across the backs, dodging heaps of garbage, sheds and huts, and gradually heading for Second Street. For nearly a minute he lost sight of his quarry, and then a horseman emerged farther down the street and spurred away towards the east.

It was Rudge all right. He was mounted on the same big dun with the black mane and tail. He was out of range of a revolver, too. Henry paused with his face flushed, recovering his breath. He thought about the latest development. How could he cut Bella,

Bill and Ike out of his life after what they had done for him that day? And yet he still felt that he had to. After all, the running feud between Rudge and himself could only have one outcome. Barring treachery, it could only end in a gun duel to the death.

A possible solution to his present dilemma occurred to him. He went off down Second Street, making a detour back to the place where they had taken the meal and stabled their horses. If he went off, mounted up, in hot pursuit, he wouldn't have to explain to his friends about another parting.

At the livery, he soon had out the palomino and paid his bill. By a circuitous route, he avoided Marshal Kelly, as well as his friends. He made good progress clear of the settlement and out towards the east. The place where Rudge had turned south-eastward towards the border with New Mexico, and probably Stillwater, was not hard to find.

But the fugitive killer was well

mounted, and by sundown the hard-ridden palomino was still some distance behind. Henry had another surprise when he awakened an hour after dawn. Bella, Ike and Bill rode into his camp, as if catching up with him was an everyday occurrence.

When breakfast was nicely under way, Bella had a revelation or two to make. 'Back there in Junction, Big Maria revealed that Kent's pardners were men called Jim Revere an' Frenchy Morelle. At one time, along with Long Tom, they were associates of one Dan Moran, my unlamented husband, in Silver City, Colorado. Rudge talked of Moran to them. That was how he managed to get them to ambush you so easily.'

Henry eyed her thoughtfully through the smoke of the fire. Seeing his interest, she left her perch on a flat rock and moved around to join him.

'Bella, if this news has shaken you up at all, I'm truly sorry. You ought to put Moran strictly into the background of your mind, forget him, an' look towards the future.'

She knelt on one knee beside him. 'Oh, I have done that already, Henry,' she explained. 'Moran talk doesn't bother me a great deal. I'm only tellin' you this to make you understand that I'm involved in what you're doin' an' to make you understand that you can't keep me out any longer. Besides, I've seen Big Maria's face since she was bereaved, an' that means somethin', too.'

Henry examined her afresh, noting the tight little dimples in her cheeks and the righteous anger reflected in bright patches of colour. Her green eyes flashed at him. They drew closer. This time he was the instigator of the kiss, but some little time later he asked himself how a man could be thinking of love when he had murder in his heart.

He was troubled by his conscience when he moved on again.

10

Never, for a long time, had Jerry Rudge partaken of so much arduous exercise as when he struggled to keep ahead of Henry Walton on the long ride from Chaparral to Stillwater. Long before he was in sight of his destination he was saddle sore. Fear kept him moving. Fear of Henry, and fear that his own wrongdoings would catch up with him.

Rudge saw Stillwater as a haven. He reminded himself many times of the far-reaching influence of his father, Dector Hector Rudge, and what people would do as a favour to the doctor, in exchange for recent help in the past when members of families were stricken with some dread disease.

Around nine o'clock one morning, the fugitive pulled up by a stream and did his level best to make himself look respectable before entering his home town. He shaved with cold water, cut some of the long ends from the hair of his head, and finally trimmed his moustache and finger nails. He punched out the crown of his black hat, dusted it carefully with a cloth, pinched it again at the crown and stuck it back on his head.

Looking towards the distant cluster of buildings with the eddying smoke above it, he wondered how the townsfolk would react to him. Several months had gone by since they last saw him. They would remember him all right, but would they look upon him with a friendly eye? After all, he had on several occasions given them cause to wish him elsewhere.

And there was the matter of the doctor himself. Blood was thick, of course, but it did not mean that the ageing sawbones would welcome the particular problem which Jerry was bringing home to him on this occasion. Jerry felt certain that Henry would keep right on coming, all the way into Stillwater, even though he had left under a cloud some three years previously. Until the tragedy which had sent Henry away with a bad reputation, the Walton boy had been very popular. Was it possible he could have his reputation restored?

The dun carried him steadily nearer to the town. Soon everyday sounds carried to his ears. The smith, in one of the end buildings, was busy at his forge. The steady blows of a hammer on an anvil carried out to the newcomer, who experienced a moment of pure fright.

How would it be if the townsfolk refused to make allowances for him any more, when old Doc Rudge asked them? What if the old man's reputation and prestige had gone by the board now? Many years had elapsed since Hector Rudge's image was likened to that of a saint. The town had been ravaged by smallpox. Rudge had shaken off his own illness, and worked himself round the clock for days on end to help others. Even when his own wife had succumbed, he still fought on, struggling to save life. He had aged in their midst in a very short time.

One of the first men to set eyes on Jerry this visit was the parson. He pulled up short, coming out of the livery near the end of the street, and surveyed the returned prodigal with steady, shaded eyes.

Jerry touched his hat. 'Mornin', preacher. It sure is good to be back in town, an' to know you are well an' takin' care of your flock. By the way, do you happen to know where my father is?'

'Can't say that I do, Jerry. As you remarked, I'm fit and well. I don't have much reason for seein' the doctor in the daytime. Mind you, he won't be idle. He'll be out visitin' some place or another by this time. I imagine we'll meet again, if you're stayin' long.'

The parson nodded curtly and crossed the dirt of the street without waiting to find out how long a stay the young man planned. Jerry felt that he had been snubbed. Twenty yards farther along the street, he came abreast of his favourite saloon, but by then several notables had spotted him, and two or three influential women.

He turned his attention away from the batwings and made a great play of solicitude when he saw a slightly overdressed woman in a wide skirt, a ribboned hat and carrying a gay parasol.

'Why, young Mr Rudge, isn't it? The doctor's son. How nice to see you back in town.'

The woman in question, who was the wife of the wealthiest merchant in town, lowered her parasol the better to see him. Jerry thought that if he survived one or two meetings of this calibre his image might be materially improved in the town. Eventually, he steered the conversation around to his father's present whereabouts.

'Let me see,' the woman pondered, tapping the parasol shaft against a dainty shoe, 'I think a person in my husband's store reckoned the doctor was drivin' out to Rattler Creek, that new settlement where the nesters are. You'll know it, of course. Some scrawny child fallen off a hoss, or somethin'.'

Rudge terminated the conversation as soon as he could after that. He felt that he would have a good chance to talk to his father undisturbed if he rode out quickly and escorted the old man back to town. He made much of tipping his hat to ladies, and calling cheery greetings to the well-to-do, but as soon as he was clear of town on the new track which led to the populated part of the creek he pushed the dun as though it was badly in need of exercise. After this, he didn't want to meet anyone until he had said his piece to his father.

⋆ ⋆ ⋆

Hector Rudge finished splinting a spindly leg belonging to an old nester's grandson and declined payment for it.

'Pay me when you're good an' rich,

an' your sons are buckin' for Mayor, Mort,' he suggested with a laugh.

The grandmother insisted on his drinking a mug of coffee, but that was as far as she could detain him. Out in the yard, the oldest son of the old man was standing by the head of the sleek bay between the shafts of the buckboard. While the doctor had been busy, the animal had been groomed, watered and lightly fed.

Stillwater people knew the value of a good horse to a man in the doctor's profession. They always treated it as well as the sawbones himself. Rudge shook hands with the adults, pressed small coins into the hands of the injured boy and a small girl toddler, and finally hurried to the conveyance with his bag in his hand.

At fifty-one, he looked to be of indeterminate age. His stovepipe hat hid a good head of fair whitish hair. The maroon cravat, which set off his sober business suit, hid the slight scrawniness at his neck. He was a little above average height, and possibly twenty pounds heavier than his healthy average. Steel-rimmed spectacles aided his shortening sight, and his rheumatism was not troubling him on this particular day.

The doctor tossed his bag on to the seat of the vehicle and followed it, declining a boost from Jake Nuttall, who was more than willing. He exchanged a few pleasant words with the son and heir, and kicked off the brake, moving away in a flurry of dust. Just once he looked back, and waved. He was comparing old Mort's heir with Jeremy, his own.

He sighed.

The bay carried him past another small homestead, and turned without prompting to the ford. The shaft horse liked the coolness of the water. It was half-way across the ford when the doctor became aware of the horseman awaiting his arrival in the shallows on the opposite side.

His heart lurched as soon as he had

identified the unexpected arrival as his son, Jeremy. There was no warmth when he returned the wave, and when the buck-board drew abreast the sweating dun, the medical man made no attempt to stop.

He murmured: 'It's good to know you're well, son. I suppose I can't deny that.'

Jerry touched his hat. 'Father, I'm sorry to barge back into your life like this, but the fact is, I'm in trouble.'

He was going on to say that the trouble was serious, but his father did not give him the chance. As the buck-board and dun horse climbed out on the townward side of the water, Rudge Senior started to reveal his true feelings.

'Can you ever remember any time when you were *not* in trouble? *I* can't! After that last little episode when you lamed a prize stallion, I told you I couldn't stand any more of your sort of trouble! In fact, I told you to go, an' I paid you to stay away so you wouldn't foul up my life here where I'm respected an' needed! I also told you that if you came back botherin' me the allowance would have to stop! Have you any idea of the trouble I've taken to get the allowance to any an' every old spot where you happened to be livin' it up? Have you?'

Jerry cleared his throat. This far, everything had gone as he had expected. 'Well, Pa, you certainly have the right to be good an' angry, but when you are more yourself you'll see that I have come home an' that I expected the allowance to stop.'

Fifty yards bumped by under them before the doctor asked the obvious question. 'Are you tellin' me that this latest trouble is so serious you had to give up your regular allowance?'

'It's jest that, Pa. My life is in danger.'

'Who an' what manner of people have you been tormentin' that they seek to threaten your life?'

Jerry was slow to answer. He felt sure that his father still had some affection for him, but this far none of it had shown. Perhaps if he went a little slower . . .

'There was an accident at a circus a long way away from here. Some of the outfit caught fire. The proprietor thought I was to blame, an' he's seekin' revenge. That's all!'

'If you had set fire to a circus, or been responsible for such a thing, almost any man with spirit might come after you with a gun! Was anyone hurt?'

'I — I don't think anyone was killed as a result of the fire.'

'Didn't stop long enough to find out, huh? Well, it figures. I've known I had that kind of a son for a long time now. Not that I take any pleasure out of such knowledge. Seein' as how this — this accident happened a long distance from here, I don't suppose I'd know the owner of the business?'

Jerry would have liked to have ducked this question, but he knew he could not. Brusquely prompted, he admitted that the circus owner was

Henry Walton. The colour of the doctor's cheeks suggested that his blood pressure was striving to get out of control.

'I knew you'd be shocked, Pa, when you heard the fellow's name. But you must remember the circumstances when Henry left town! You'll allow that when he's riled he's a difficult man to deal with! You *will* help me, won't you?'

'Have done with blackenin' Henry's character, son, or I'll see you run out of town! You hear me? Sure, I know the full details of what happened when Henry left town. He went away, forsakin' this place he was brought up in, as a special favour to me! He didn't cause the death of any poor little innocent Mexican kid! He went away to shield the real culprit, an' we both know who that was. Don't we?'

Jerry had turned pale. Perhaps in asking this latest favour of his father, he had asked too much. 'You knew about the burnin' of the Mex shack all this time, an' you never challenged me with it, Pa? How come you kept it locked up inside of you like that?'

The doctor idly flicked his whip over the back of his horse. He was slow in answering. 'What good would it have done? That wasn't the first time anyone made a big sacrifice to keep you out of serious trouble. Neither was it the last. An' here you are askin' me to believe that young Henry is chasin' you all the way from . . . where did you say the fire took place?'

'Chaparral, Utah territory.'

'All the way from Chaparral, Utah? Are you sure you didn't set fire to his circus, Jeremy?'

'I'm quite sure I didn't set fire to it, father,' the son answered, dry-throated.

The doctor studied his eyes and general expression and had a suspicion that Jeremy was implicated, even if he didn't use the match or torch. Almost a furlong went by before the father felt like discussing the matter further.

'What makes you think Henry will come ridin' into a town where he's thought to be guilty of a child's death, jest to shoot you?'

'He's been on my tail for days now. Only a good hoss kept me out of his clutches. Believe me, Pa, I'm not wrong in assessin' the situation. Henry felt a lot for that circus, an' he's strong for a blood-lettin'!'

The sawbones yawned and sighed. Less than two hundred yards from town, it looked as if he had nothing further to say. Jerry began to get agitated again.

'You don't want this shootin' any more than *I* do! You still have influence in the town. You could use it to have Henry put off, I'm sure you could! The folks need you jest as much as they ever did!'

'But I wouldn't forsake them if they weren't helpful over you, son. Don't make any mistakes there. An' understand this. I'm not goin' to bring Henry to any harm. I'll see what I can do about delayin' him, but only on condition you keep right on ridin' out of town. That's my condition, see?'

The buckboard was stopped in a flurry of dust. Its driver dipped into the pocket of his suit and brought out a fold of dollar bills. Roughly halving the money, he handed over one wad, which Jeremy took rather nervously. Rudge Senior's expression had an air of finality about it.

'Don't I get to see home, not for an hour, even?'

The doctor shook his head. 'No, you don't. You go now, an' you keep goin'. Head for the Rio Grande. Goodbye, son.'

The bay in the shafts leapt forward and Jerry was left behind, open-mouthed. He had never seen his father act so forthrightly before. Reluctantly, he turned the dun's head and moved away from town again, heading out towards the east.

Already he was making calculations about the future.

11

Young Rudge's pursuers rested some three miles farther from Stillwater on the day before the fugitive finally made town. All of them knew that they would make town the following morning, and that Jerry had contrived to stay ahead of them. They knew they would have troubles. Henry had turned in early, and after sleep had claimed him, Bella and the other two had things to discuss. They were very firm in their resolve, and it was not until the normal breakfast hour that their plans began to take shape.

Henry drank copiously of the coffee from the smaller of two pots. He never knew while he was drinking that only he was using that pot. Bella, Bill and Ike, all acting rather oddly, took their beverage from the larger pot and awaited developments.

Henry kept yawning as he hunkered on a low rock and drained his mug. He glanced into the sky and studied the position of the sun, which was still mounting, but slowly.

'Sure enough an' that sun's gettin' to rise early,' he opined. 'My head an' the condition of my brain tells me it's two hours earlier than the sun knows about. I can't understand it.'

The trio with him exchanged glances. 'If you feel sleepy, Henry, ain't no reason why we shouldn't all rest up for another hour or so before we make the last ride of our journey. After all, there's nothin' to be gained now by hurryin'.' This was Bella's suggestion.

'Sure is a lot of truth in what you're sayin', Bella,' Henry replied, massaging his temples. 'All the same, what has still to be done ain't pleasant, an' the more it gets put off the unpleasanter it will seem. So I'll jest have to make the effort an' get me into my saddle, come what may.'

Before he could get up, Bella moved

over and sat beside him on the same rock. A minute later, his head sagged towards her. She took a gentle hold of him, and kept him up until his eyes closed again.

'He ain't goin' to like what we did to him, boys, but there was no other way. We agreed on that, didn't we?'

Ike and Bill nodded, and helped her to stretch Henry out and put him back under his blanket. Bella busied herself about the camp. Every now and then she shot sharp glances at her fellow conspirators.

'All right, so it was my idea to dope his coffee, but it ain't the end of the world!' she protested. 'After all, we did agree that we couldn't let him get himself dubbed a murderer for a no-good jasper like Jerry Rudge.'

The girl straightened up, sticking her hands on her hips. 'If you boys don't fancy going on into town to do the dirty work, I'd be glad to take your places.'

Bill Trask coloured up. 'You know

why we can't let you soil your hands with that kind of work, Bella. Don't keep rilin' us up. We don't like takin' advantage of Henry, is all. So give us time. We'll be goin'.'

'I've got a feelin' there's a coach or somethin' on the way towards town,' Ike explained. 'If, as you say, the doc's sympathisers try to stop us goin' in, maybe it wouldn't be a bad thing for one of us to beg a lift, make it look as if we're jest ordinary trail riders, or somethin'.'

'I'm goin' to try an' pass myself off as an ordinary prospector, takin' only the mule with me,' Bill informed them. 'If you want to try gettin' in by coach, Ike, it's okay by me, but you have to go alone.'

This was agreed on. Ike hastened to the trail and checked with a spy-glass that a coach was, indeed, on the way. He gathered his few useful belongings together, including a saddle, and left his pinto in the charge of Bella. The parting was a brief but emotional one.

* * *

On trail, the driver of the coach looked rather doubtfully at the small man with nowhere to put his saddle. He pulled up with an obvious show of reluctance, on account of his being an hour or so behind schedule.

'All right, Shorty, make with the hard-luck story, an' make it short!'

Ike explained how it was difficult to get ponies small enough to accommodate him. His, he told them, had broken a limb. He'd had to shoot it, and now he couldn't make much of himself until he reached a town. He did not take up much room, and he could pay for the lift.

The shotgun guard had his thoughts centred very largely on certain creature comforts which were awaiting him in town. He wanted to be on his way with the least delay and inconvenience. A well-to-do traveller on the inside finally swayed the balance in Ike's favour and made it possible for him to scramble up into the luggage boot at the rear.

People started to show a special interest in the coach as soon as it entered the first street. For fifty yards, Ike played possum, making out he was asleep in the boot. The curious ones eyed him and lost interest. He looked altogether too ordinary. Even his lack of stature did not show in that posture. Outside the hotel, the coach finally stopped. Ike was alert and ready. He hopped off without drawing attention to himself and skipped around the back of a cart before disappearing down an alley.

The crew expressed surprise for perhaps ten seconds after finding him missing. They promptly forgot about him, writing him off as an ordinary free-loader. In the nearest eating house, the little man showed an interest in the overworked proprietor, who had been talking of retiring from business for a twelvemonth. For his sympathy, Ike was well fed. He received permission to leave his saddle in the back room, and he also learned quite a bit about the movements of Rudge.

Every other person was saying how the doctor's son had put in a brief appearance, and then, to his father's surprise, had moved right on through towards the east. Ike went into a saloon, where he checked that the information was correct. He believed it, and wondered if he would not have done better to have had his pony with him, after all.

He decided to use his initiative and move a little farther east. After all, Bill and anyone else who came into town would soon learn what he had. They would guess that, if he didn't show up, he would have gone on.

Having made up his mind, he went out of his way to renew acquaintance with the coach crew, who were telling anyone who cared to listen how they had to go right on again, on account of some bigshot from back east who could not afford the time to sleep in Stillwater.

'Whiskies for the driver an' guard, please!' he requested.

While they were getting over their surprise, he slipped each of them a silver dollar, and apologised for not having thanked them for the lift. As their brief time slipped away, he availed himself of the bottle and filled up their glasses again.

'Gents, I want you to take it that this liquor was freely given. All the same, I'd be obliged if you could allow me to travel a little farther east, in the boot, where I was before. Think you could accommodate me?'

He was so serious that they had to laugh. Ike did not mind being laughed at so long as he got what he wanted. Shortly before the passengers took their seats again, the guard shifted two valises out of the boot, restacking them on the roof. This made it possible for Ike to get farther into the boot, and thus attract even less attention.

Even while he was in the boot, he heard men talking in lowered tones about how they were planning to delay Henry Walton, in the event of his hitting town in the near future. The coach crew heard about it, but they did not seem to be greatly interested.

* * *

Some ten furlongs east of Stillwater, Jerry Rudge waited in a kind of lay-by, fringed with stones. It was his intention, if possible, to get himself taken aboard the coach. He wanted a change of motion, and at the same time he had to rest his dun. For the last few miles before Stillwater it had shown signs of flagging, due to the arduous work it had been called upon to do in keeping ahead of Henry Walton.

Caution was now a natural part of the lone rider's make-up. Before he showed himself, or even gave an inkling of his presence, he had to be sure that Henry had not slipped Rudge sympathisers and come on straight through. From this time in his life, it seemed, he would always be checking faces. It was almost like being a criminal, a man on the run from justice. He did not realise as he thought about the situation that he fitted the part perfectly.

In avoiding acquaintances after leaving his father, he had not been able to avail himself of everyday information in the town. For instance, he was not at all sure that the coach would come. He knew the driver and the guard of old. If they could possibly help it, they always tried to spend the night in Stillwater before going on again.

He wondered whether they would make it on this occasion, when his future more or less rested on the decision. His nerves were troubling him by this time. He slackened his saddle and rolled himself a smoke, but not before he had spilled two lots of makings on the ground. When the smoke was drawing, he paced backwards and forwards, screened from the trail by the rocks, and wondering about the immediate future.

His father's decision to send him straight on out again had shaken him. So had the old man's knowledge about the Mexican family's fire disaster. Jerry had taken a few fingers of strong liquor on that day when he went out camping with Henry. He could not sleep, whereas Henry had slept only too well. Jerry's restlessness, as always, had led him into trouble.

He had taken brands from the fire and hurled them in different directions. Inevitably, with his outlook on life, he had to have a target. The Mexicans' shack seemed the very place. He believed that they were all out, visiting town, but he did not take the trouble to find out before he started to endanger the property. Fire had always intrigued him. He had taken a fiendish glee in pitching a burning brand through an open window.

The drapes and other inflammable materials had soon ignited. He had stood at a safe distance and watched them burn. Soon the whole of the building was gushing smoke. Farther off, Henry slept on, totally unaware of the situation until it was too late to be of assistance.

The child had cried when it was too late. Probably it had been sleeping soundly, alone in the house. Jerry got as far as the gallery, but the smoke swept him back. That, and the knowledge that he might be found out and severely punished for his guilt. He cleared out rather quickly; too quickly, in fact, for Henry to see him there when the smoke and crackle brought him to the spot.

Jerry saw the whole scene as he paced about that uneven arena of rocks. It haunted him worse than ever before. *But how could his father have known all about his guilt and kept quiet about it for so long?*

He stopped pacing in an effort to break his train of thought. In that he was successful, because before he could pace any more he heard unmistakeable sounds which suggested the coach was coming through, after all. He took certain steps to make sure that he would remain undiscovered until he was ready to reveal himself.

The coach looked very ordinary as it rocked towards the spot. He held himself in and used a spy-glass in an effort to see the faces of the inside passengers. His heart was thumping, but it all seemed innocent enough. And then it was past, and he was seeing the rear view. He rose to his feet with the glass still to his eye. The sun glinted on metal. He gasped, and saw the dwarf for the first time, toying with his lethal throwing knives and momentarily distracted from his survey of the trail and its fringes by the weapons in his hand.

Scarcely daring to breathe, Rudge sank back out of sight. He was shaking and the glass was still against his eye a minute later. In spite of the invidiousness of his position, he had lost the will to go on farther east. The sight of the dwarf had struck terror into him. He felt that he would recover his nerve, but for the present he would have to backtrack to somewhere in Stillwater. He could not face his enemies in the open.

The dun protested as he tightened the saddle girth. He almost overdid it, but soon he was mounted up again and striving to get back into the town without showing himself in the obvious places.

The whinny of protest had carried farther than he thought.

12

The heat inside the blanket was the reason for Henry finally shaking off the sleep which had been specially induced. The sun was well over his head, and although his head was still muzzy, he felt guilty; like a child who has overslept and become late for a big occasion.

He called out hoarsely: 'Hey, Bella, what in tarnation's goin' on around here?'

The girl left off working on the horses, swallowed hard, and came across to him to admit her fault. 'You slept a little longer than the others on account of your coffee was strong, Henry. I'm to blame for that. I doped you in a womanly effort to stop you from runnin' into serious trouble.'

Henry rose to his feet, bootless. He swelled with anger. 'You did this to me, Bella? You took the liberty? Lettin' Bill an' Ike go on without me to tackle what was rightly *my* business?'

He seized her by the shoulders and held her close to him. Her eyes gradually swam as his grip hurt her. 'Your business an' mine,' she retorted. 'I wouldn't like to have to perform in front of the public tonight, because I'll have bruises on my shoulders.'

He let go the shoulders, but still contrived to have an arm around her body, so that she could not go off.

'Did you think I wasn't a match for Jerry Rudge? Was that it?'

Bella sighed and slumped against him. Angered as he was, he smelled the fresh smell of her hair. It occurred to him, in a sudden flash of insight, that if he parted with her now, for good, he would miss her intolerably. His mind was groping towards town, wondering what had happened, or was happening, to Bill and Ike. For a moment or two, however, he was unable to break the spell of this beautiful, desirable young woman whom he loved.

Unaware of the change within him, Bella started to explain.

'Of course you're a match for Jerry. In everythin' except villainy. The trouble with men is that when they get really worked up they don't see straight. All the time we're concerned about you. If you kill him, you'll have his death on your conscience for the rest of your life. Don't you understand?'

'No. Right at this moment I don't. If I have to shoot him, I'll do it in the approved way, givin' him a fair chance to kill me. That's the rattlesnake code, as I know it, an' I don't see any reason to be ashamed of actin' by it. By the way, did Dan Moran ever have his plans seriously interfered with by you?'

Bella was not as hurt as she might have been. In the matter of her marriage, Jerry Rudge was better informed than Henry. Her eyes sought his, with an infinite tenderness.

'I never had the chance to interfere where he was concerned,' she murmured.

'There you go, talkin' in riddles

again,' Henry blustered.

He allowed himself to be taken by the hand, back to a rock where they had previously sat to eat food. Without embroidering at all, Bella explained to him how her marriage had been over almost before it had begun. The girl's explanation calmed him far more than her excuse for the doping.

Ten more minutes slipped away while they held hands in silence.

'I'm glad you saw fit to tell me what you did, Bella. Jest one thing still puzzles me right now. I heard in a roundabout way that you was a sort of mail-order bride, that you answered some newspaper advertisement put in by this fellow Moran, in Silver City. Now, your life is your own, of course, but why did you have to go off like that an' marry a man you hadn't ever met, when you could have had almost any eligible young fellow in Stillwater?'

'That's one little secret I'm going to keep from you for a while longer, Henry,' Bella murmured, with a smile.

'Do you want to risk takin' another cup of coffee from me, or are you goin' into town jest the way you are?'

He kissed her, and took a cup with her. One thing he made clear, and that was she was to remain behind. At least for a while. Bella acquiesced. She knew that this might be the most critical day of her life, and Henry went some way towards assessing the depths of her feelings towards him.

He carried away with him a picture of her in his mind's eye. All shapely and lithe in a man's bottle-green shirt and a black pair of denims thrust into half-boots. Her hair, blowing loose, masked and unmasked her delicate features, and brushed away tears.

How would she pass the time while he was away?

* * *

Once out of sight of her, Henry recovered his resolution. He made a slight detour as Stillwater loomed up, so as not to betray his presence to anyone who might want to deny him access to the town. His ruse worked. He also had a small piece of luck. In detouring towards the south, he came upon Dr Rudge's buckboard and bay horse standing outside the gate of a small horse ranch belonging to a settler who had arrived five years earlier. The doctor emerged before Henry had the time to roll a smoke. The older man's joviality and energy went back on him when he saw who the rider was.

The horse rancher showed concern for the doctor's health, but Rudge came away assuring him that all was well with him.

Henry touched his hat, and nodded rather gravely, backing off the palomino so that the doctor's progress to his vehicle would not be impeded. The medical man's throat appeared to have dried out.

'Good day to you, Doctor.'

'Good day to you, too, Henry. I heard tell you were headin' back for town.

How did the folks treat you? Was it all right?'

Rudge settled himself on the seat and tucked a blanket around his legs. Henry found himself wondering how far a father with a conscience would go to help his ne'er-do-well son.

He said, 'Only Jerry could have told you I was comin', so I'm takin' it he arrived in good order. As for the other matter, no one in town attempted to delay me because this far they haven't set eyes on me. Now, sir, as to the matter of your son. I take it he has talked to you?'

'He told me a story about a burnt-down circus, an' that you were comin' hell bent to threaten his life over it. I sure didn't like the sound of that, Henry. It didn't seem like you at all!'

'Jerry paid men to set fire to the circus. He wouldn't do it himself. They also released wild animals, an' caused an accident to — to Bella Lester, who worked for me. He even attacked her in her wagon!'

Rudge paled, and then coloured up. He appeared to sway on the seat. Then he kicked off the brake and gently urged the bay forward. Henry kept pace with him, holding in the palomino.

'It — it's no use goin' on, Henry! Jerry has been an' gone! I tell you he's already left!'

'Did he tell you he paid three drifters to ambush an' kill me on the way here? An' how about poor Long Tom Brett, shot dead by Jerry's own hand in Junction?'

The doctor appeared to shrivel on the seat. He did not have the spirit to challenge any of the seemingly wild accusations worded by Henry. He polished his spectacles with an unsteady hand and wondered how this feud between Henry and Jerry would turn out. Certainly there were passions at work which an ageing doctor would find hard to check.

The bay threaded its way over new and lightly marked tracks around the south and south-east of the town.

Several minutes of silence went by, during which Henry had qualms of conscience over what he had just done to a decent, ailing old man.

'My son went on through town on my specific instructions, Henry. Right now, I'm not on call. Maybe if we rode out towards the east a little way, you'd come to believe me about his movements?'

Henry had spent himself for the time being. He professed himself agreeable to ride in the suggested direction, but gave no guarantee as to his behaviour in the event of Jerry's being overtaken. Rudge had to go along with that. Since the coach had gone through, two carts and a bunch of riders had left for the east. The first examination of the trail east showed how difficult the search might be.

In the days when he had lived in Stillwater, Henry had always shown the doctor the greatest respect, especially since he had been left parentless. Now, he had doubts. He was surprised when the older man read his thoughts.

'I know what you're thinkin', Henry. You believe I may be leadin' you away from my boy. Well, such is not the case. You've been badly treated in the past, but not by me, except on that one occasion when you did me a service. To the best of my knowledge, Jerry is up ahead of us somewhere.'

Henry rode on, silent and morose. His thoughts explored in all directions. He wondered how Ike and Bill were making out, and how long Bella's patience would hold her to the camp outside of town. He fixed his eyes on the trail ahead, marked off a landmark, and decided that would be the limit of his trek east, failing further positive evidence that Jerry was ahead.

Fifty yards short of the outcrop, they slowed as the trail grew steeper. Seemingly out of nowhere, but really out of a small plateau on the north side, shrouded by rocks and overhanging vegetation, came a brief sharp whistle. Little Ike's head showed up over a rock almost at once. He had his hat pushed back, and his face showed signs of perspiration.

'Doggone it, Henry, am I pleased to see you? Right now, I was figurin' on havin' to walk all the way back into town, or waitin' till somebody came along goin' that way! How did you get on in your search? No hard feelings about the rest of us startin' out ahead of you?'

'Everything's okay between us, Ike. This gent is Doctor Rudge, the father of the man we're seekin'.'

Encouraged by Henry, Ike nodded to the doctor, but the skin across his bony skull appeared to have tightened. His breath entered and left his body harshly. Rudge perceived that the small man was really upset by the mention of Jerry. He shuddered, and wondered how many more righteously indignant folk there were on his son's trail.

'If you were headin' this way after young Rudge, you can think again. I've turned him back.'

Prompted by Henry, Ike started to explain how he had taken a lift in the boot of the coach specially to get after the runaway. He pointed to sign at the back of the rocks, and the place where the single rider had left the small arena and gone back to town.

'It was hearin' his hoss whinny put me on to him. I didn't exactly set eyes on him, but he must have seen me on the look-out. No other man would have had reason to back off after examinin' the coach an' passengers. Would they?'

The doctor declined to answer. He indicated that the horseless dwarf should take a ride with him on the buck-board. Henry turned his palomino around. Slowly, they returned down-trail towards the town. A hundred yards short, the vehicle stopped. Dr Rudge's eyes spoke volumes, but his lips were silent. Not so Henry's.

'Here's where we part, sir. I'm still chasin' your son, but I want you to know he'll have a fair chance, if it comes to guns. I'll not treat him the way he treats others.'

'You may die, if you fight fairly,' Ike murmured, as he left the buckboard and scrambled up behind his one-time boss.

The doctor drove on. His muteness spoke volumes.

13

Oddly enough, it was the doctor who drove straight on, up the main street of town. Henry and Ike, both mounted on the same horse, moved over towards the north-east, seeking out the doctor's residence on its own private eminence.

There, they were due for a surprise, but theirs was scarcely as great as that of the lounging lawman who was whiling away his time by swinging gently on a hung settee well back on the verandah.

Town Marshal Russ Walker had held office in Still-water for a great many years. He was forty-six years of age. He and his wife had but one child, a daughter. It was their considered opinion that Dr Rudge had, by his skill and devotion to the child, saved her life when she had pneumonia. Russ had never forgotten this. His wife made it her business to remind him of it from time to time.

In appearance, the peace officer was unprepossessing. He had a red, pockmarked face, to some extent screened by a greying moustache and sideburns. He was a little under six feet tall and weighed twelve stones. On all except very special occasions he was seen about the town in a shabby corduroy jacket and a curly-brimmed grey stetson. This was not considered a special occasion.

As soon as he identified Henry, he whistled soundlessly through his teeth and adjusted the gunbelt around his waist. Henry had once been a thoroughly peace-loving and law-abiding young man, but if what the doctor had said happened to be the truth, then Henry was now a man to be reckoned with, and he did not mind if he was pushed into gunplay.

Walker rose to his feet and slowly crossed to the gate at the inner end of the doctor's short shingle drive. He rested his body against the gate, and nodded to the riders.

'Good day to you, Henry. It's been a long time. Did you have any special reason for droppin' by at this time?'

Henry gave Ike an arm and lowered him to the ground. 'Howdy, Marshal. You know as well as any other man in this gossip-ridden town why I'm here. I'm lookin' for Jerry Rudge. It would save the pair of us a whole lot of trouble if you'd tell me straight away whether he's in the house back there.'

Walker was angry, and a little on edge. He had certain cronies in the town who were supposed to have stopped Henry's forward progress to the Rudge house, in the event that he entered town, as he was supposed to do. They, it seemed, had failed in their duty. This was one situation which could go any way at all, so he thought.

'If he was in there, he'd have every right to be there. But he ain't. He's been along to see his father an' left town again. I believe he went towards the east.'

Ike remarked: 'That was the way he started out, but he came back again. I figure I frightened him.'

Walker was surprised and nonplussed by this fighting utterance from the undersized man. Henry added that they had just left the doctor, who had continued his drive towards the centre of town.

He asked again: 'Are you quite sure Jerry isn't in that building, Marshal?'

'Certain sure. I've been here for quite some time. Didn't figure to meet you here, though, I must admit.'

'Well,' Henry continued lightly, 'I guess you're still honest enough to speak the truth, so I'll look somewhere else. I feel I ought to warn you, though, that if you figure on intervenin' on Jerry's behalf you'll be sidin' with a murderer, an' that won't look any too good for you when the reports start tricklin' into town about Jerry's latest doings.'

Walker toyed with the gate fastening. 'Henry, I'd find it awful easy to take offence at what you say an' your attitude, but I don't want to be that way. I won't ask you to substantiate what you've jest said, either. Tell you what I will do, though. I'll run out my hoss an' ride along with you, help you to search.'

Henry gave him a hard smile, and suggested that he made up his own mind about such a course of action. Ike seemed restless. When he had Henry's attention, he explained that he wanted to locate Bill, and to pick up his saddle at the eating house. Henry approved the idea, and said he would come looking for them later.

Ike went off and soon Marshal Walker was back in the saddle of a brown and white paint which had been idling around the back of the house.

'I've covered a certain amount of ground south of the town. Right now I'd like to look farther north.'

Walker nodded and sniffed. Side by side, they inspected the outlying hamlets and isolated shacks. Gradually, after ninety minutes' riding, and with the marshal asking questions, they came slowly closer into town. As they did so, the peace officer straightened with relief, while Henry smouldered internally.

Some of his bitterness was bound to show itself before they parted. It was long in coming to the surface, but when it appeared there was no mistaking it. Three o'clock showed by the clock on the front of the big saloon. All the way down Main Street people were shaking off the sleepiness of early afternoon and beginning to take an interest in the affairs of the day.

Henry's straight figure acted like a magnet to their eyes. Seeing him with the marshal, many people wondered if Walker had grabbed him and was taking him to the peace office to lay some charge against him. Those who had been awake all through *siesta* time, on account of having been given small amounts of money to watch for Henry, wondered how he had gone past them without their knowing.

Walker kept nodding and smiling easily, first on the one hand and then on the other. It was this behaviour which finally made Henry boil over.

'Marshal, you must be feelin' good! Smirkin' up an' down these voters who put you in office, an' you settin' yourself up as the protector of a murderer, a fire-raiser, a causer of accidents to innocent young women, an' who has no respect for the weaker sex! What manner of man do you think you're shelterin'? Has the law gone off its head?'

Walker checked the pinto, short of his office. 'Now you're talkin' like I expected, Henry! I don't have to take that sort of talk from the likes of you! What makes you think you are so almighty respectable? Folks in this town can remember back to the time when you left, an' you left in a hurry, didn't you?'

Henry kneed the palomino nearer as the listeners and watchers thickened around them. In all the street, he could see only two friendly faces, and for once they seemed to be looking the other way. He did not care. This was his fight, and he intended to fight it any way it developed.

'I did leave in a hurry, Walker, an' that — in your suspicious mind — makes me the killer of a small Mexican girl who couldn't save herself from a fire! Doesn't it? Do you ever think back to that time? I was the only man in Stillwater who tried to save her! When I left town, Stillwater thought what it wanted to think. It made me the scapegoat because it was ashamed of what happened! I was condemned in the eyes of all you folks left behind! But you never did have a shred of evidence that *I* set fire to the Mex shack! Did you ever dwell on that fact?'

Walker was slow to answer. All round about, though, people were muttering and fuming and only waiting for a lead from somebody to cut Henry down to size.

* * *

A few minutes earlier, Bella Lester had approached town from the west. Her patience had given out. She knew the man she loved was in deep trouble and she could not let anything bad happen to him while she hovered around a fire just a short distance from the settlement.

She had with her, in addition to her own sorrel mare, Ike's small pinto and Bill's claybank. She had broken camp, not thinking that they would ever go back to the same place. As she approached the end of the buildings she could hear the angry shouting from a distance.

She dismounted and climbed up an arched welcome sign, using a ladder which had been propped against it and forgotten. The spy-glass showed her how things were going. Henry's patience had given out. He was saying harsh things to the peace officer which could only recoil back on his own head.

She feared for him. In this mood he was so unlike the self-disciplined master of the circus, the man she had so admired.

While she was still at the top of the ladder, and undecided as to her best course of action, someone tapped the foot of the ladder and made her look down. It was a rather simple young man, a livery hand. He was in his thirties, although he still looked like a big, overfed boy in his late teens.

'Shucks, Miss Bella, I never did hope to see you on top of a ladder in this two-hoss town! How come you're back here when everybody said you wouldn't show up no more?'

Seeing the fellow helped Bella to a course of action. She clambered down the rungs with a forced smile on her face. 'Barty, it's good to see you. Right now I don't have the time to explain why I'm back here. I could do with help. Do you think you could do a small favour for me, if I gave you a dollar?'

'Yowee, Miss Bella, I sure would like to help. I'd consider it a special pleasure, seein' as how you singled out little me to do this job for you when Main Street's topped to overflowin' with folks lookin' for somethin' to use their energy on! What — what was it you wanted me to do?'

Bella slipped him the silver coin. 'Put it in your belt, Barty, an' listen good. I want you to take this pinto an' the claybank, an' hand them over to two men you'll find at the back of the crowd up there. One of them is awful short, about so high, an' the other hombre has a big mule with him. You'll pick 'em out all right.

'When you do get in touch with them, I want you to give them a message from me. I hope you can remember. Tell them to stay real close to Henry. Can you think on that? I've got a bit of visitin' to do myself, an' I'll see them later! That's all the message, Barty, so take the ponies an' go, 'cause they might need them real soon. I'll see you again! Goodbye!'

Barty lingered over his farewell, but

he left in a businesslike way, desperately keen to carry out Bella's wishes. For her part, she scrambled a little higher on the ladder, until she could see over the heads of the tall people on her end of the crowd.

Marshal Walker was making his answer to Henry's jibes. He threw back his head and talked so that all present could hear.

'Walton, you've come back here full of fire an' threatening talk! You've run the name of our doctor through the mud, an' all because of a whole lot of things you say his son did out of town! We don't like the way you talk, and as far as I'm concerned I'm goin' to make sure you don't disturb the peace unduly! Have you finished speechifyin' now?'

Henry chuckled rather grimly. His brows rose in fine arches against his forehead, as he perceived Bill and Ike, both now mounted up on horses, and pushing their way towards him.

'Why don't you ask Doctor Rudge

whether he believes these charges I've made against his son? You could also ask him about the other business, about the burnin' of the Mexicans' hut! If you wanted to lay bare the truth, but you don't!'

Bill Trask, from ten yards away, unseated his big, undented hat and replaced it. 'Marshal, everythin' Henry Walton has said here this afternoon is true. I can vouch for it. So can my ridin' partner here, Ike Bird. So quit dredgin' up sympathy for a no-good who don't deserve it, an' if you have any guts try an' put things to rights!'

Walker seemed startled by the reappearance of Little Ike. Bill's words had nettled him rather badly. It was to Bill, when he spoke again.

'Mister, you ought to have lived long enough in Uncle Sam's country to know that a fellow ain't guilty until he's proven that way!'

He was going on to say that he didn't care very much about the unsubstantiated charges against Jerry Rudge, but

Henry cut in and made his words sound ludicrous.

'Lands sakes, Marshal, you know you don't believe that! You believe there's one law for Jerry Rudge an' another for Henry Walton! Ain't that so? Haven't you jest said as much?'

Thus verbally outwitted, Marshal Walker lost his temper. 'Git! You an' your sidekicks, all, Walton! Git out of town before I soil my cells with you!'

He pointed towards the west end of town. Most of the assembled men and women began to hustle the three towards that direction. One or two, however, the types who like to develop a small matter into a large one, grabbed for the three riders' guns. Walker showed no surprise at this. In fact, he encouraged it. Henry clenched his fists, but he submitted to having his guns taken. Bill and Ike, both fuming at the indignity, did the same.

Out they went in an untidy heap of horses and men. Their guns, minus their bullets, were tossed out after them by the angry mob. Ike still had his throwing knives which he carried in a bag hanging down his back under the black vest.

'You want I should leave one or two souvenirs, Henry?'

Knowing what he meant, Henry was slow to answer. Eventually, he shook his head. 'No, don't bother. Most of the folks ranged against us don't understand what it's all about. We'll give them time to cool down, an' then gather up our hardware. I have a feelin' that we shall still need it before this trouble is over. By the way, how did you boys come to get possession of your horses?'

Explanations started, and soon the thoughts of all three had turned to Bella and what she was planning to do.

14

Lefty Park, deputy to the Town Marshal, had also been around a long time. He did not have a clear, incisive brain, but he had the features to offput a casual drunk who planned on causing a little trouble for the peace department.

Russ Walker knew his strengths and weaknesses and used him well. Park was born with a Roman nose, but in his youth it had been spread in one of his early fist fights; which was a great pity because his father had thought that he might make a good pugilist. He also had small ears, and the cranial development behind them was quite marked. He still had his big front teeth, which a career in the prize ring might have loosened. And, nearing forty, his hair was still thick. He had a tufty fair quiff which stood straight out from his head when his hat was off.

Park had patience. He was using it when Bella went walking up to the doctor's house about an hour after the wild goings-on in Main Street. He straightened up from the side wall of the house and stood in her path, not knowing quite how to handle a woman visitor.

Bella pulled up in front of him; of necessity, not because she wanted to talk to him.

'Miss Bella?' he began slowly. 'Miss Bella Lester?'

The impatient brunette stuck a hand on her hip and quirked her mouth at him. 'That's the name I was born with, an' seein' your memory is so good, Lefty Park, perhaps you'll soon figure out I used to live in this very house!'

'That certainly had occurred to me, Miss Bella, only, you see, I had certain very definite instructions. The Marshal told me I wasn't to let in any visitors, 'cause the doctor wasn't feelin' too good an' wanted to be on his own.'

'I see how it is, Lefty, but come to your senses. Seein' as how I was raised here, you can hardly call me a visitor. So stand aside. Don't let me have to call the doctor to move you out of the way. He's got troubles enough, without havin' to make excuses for you!'

Lefty, with measured reluctance, stepped a little to one side, thinking to curb Bella's impetuosity at the same time as he gave way. She was too quick for him, however, and by the time he had lifted another foot she had gone on past, and was turning the rear corner to enter the house by the kitchen door.

The doctor was in the kitchen, slumped in his rocker near the stove and sucking on a tobacco pipe which had long since gone out. As she stepped inside, he pushed his spectacles up his nose and said, 'Oh, it's you, Bella,' as though she had never been away, and slumped back in the same position.

The girl sighed. She glanced round the room where she had spent so many happy hours. A woman came in twice a week these days to do the work which she had done all the time. She collected a match off a shelf, struck it, and held it to the pipe, as she had been wont to do in the past.

She sat in a padded chair beside him. Presently his brain cleared. 'Henry — Henry Walton said somethin' about you earlier in the day. Somethin' about how you'd been with him, in his circus. Is that so?'

'Yes, that's so. I've been with Henry for about a year an' nine months. He's been good to me, all that time, although we were never really close as people until jest recently.'

'Tell me, Bella, why did you ever take off like you did?' the doctor pleaded, cocking his head on one side.

Bella linked the fingers of her two hands and rocked herself in the padded chair. She had come specifically to enlighten the doctor as to certain unpleasant things. He had to be made to understand how things were between Jerry, Henry and his friends, and herself. In revealing facts appertaining to herself, she knew she would have to hurt the old man. But it could not be helped. He had to be made to see why Henry was behaving the way he was, and why she was backing Henry. It was for Henry's sake she was doing this, and she was prepared to hurt everybody in an attempt to safeguard him.

'It didn't have anythin' to do with you personally. You always treated me well, an' gave me a good life. But I was under pressure from another direction. From Jerry, in fact. There were times, mostly when you were out on your rounds, that he showed another side to his nature. He wandered at will, an' payin' court, in his way, to the eligible girls of the town an' district.

'I was in a special position. I have to be honest, I never did love him. Nor did I feel any sort of sisterly affection for him. But I did treat him properly. Anyways, there came a day when one of the other girls succeeded in repulsin' him, for good. Maybe her Pa got to know about Jerry's courtin' an' threatened him with a shotgun.

'Around that time, he got to pesterin' me more an' more. I didn't want to protest to you, on account of you havin' a lot of work on, an' because there would have to be a showdown of sorts within the family. Anyhow, I got a bit on the nervy side, an' you must have noticed because you sent him away to visit a distant cousin, in Silver City, Colorado.

'For a short time, it was a relief not to have him around. And then he came back, an' I could see that he was jest holding himself in. Came the day when he caught me in the stable an' I had to hit him with a chunk of wood. After that, things changed. *He* appeared to change, but I was still frightened.

'I found a paper with a Silver City advertisement in it. A man named Dan Moran, seemingly quiet, respectable an' with a decent income, wantin' a wife to share his life. I knew something had to give in the Rudge household, an' seein' Jeremy was your own flesh an' blood, I decided to go myself.

'So, encouraged by Jerry, who was actin' differently when he knew I was intent on leavin', I wrote to this Dan Moran an' made myself acquainted. You know how the correspondence developed. Jerry claimed to know the fellow, an' although I couldn't trust him in some ways, I didn't think he'd deceive me as regards matrimony. But he did.'

Doctor Rudge groaned. His voice was reduced to a whisper. 'Jerry helped to arrange your marriage, an' it was no good? How could he sink so low?'

'I think he must have hated me for keepin' him at arm's length, Doc. Anyways, shortly after the marriage I was in a position to hear my new husband conferrin' with men in another room. I overheard sufficient to know that they were outlaws an' that my husband was a close associate of theirs. I walked out on him an' I never saw him any more. This much I told to Jerry when he made contact with the circus in Chaparral.'

'Is there more to tell?' Rudge queried faintly.

'Jest a little, but it ain't pleasant. I wish I didn't have to say it, either, but it explains why I'm solidly behind Henry in this feud with Jerry. You see, I also heard it said, through that wall, that Jerry had taken money from Moran to get me out there as his wife. Moran wasn't really interested in me as a person. He simply wanted a young woman with a decent background to provide for him an aura of respectability.'

There was quietness in the room for a short while. Burned wood, settling in the stove, disturbed the man and the girl.

Rudge cleared his throat. 'An' that is the end of the tale of my son's misdeeds?'

'I think it's all you need to be told, Doc,' Bella murmured. 'What I've jest told you is the only important thing I've kept back from Henry. He's a good man, an' I think we'd make a happy marriage between us. Only this runnin' battle has to stop. I don't want Henry to kill, or to be killed. Do you understand now why I had to tell you such harrowin' things?'

The girl moved on to the old man's lap and hugged him. She knew that he understood, only too well. It was his turn to be bitter, and provided he helped with Jerry she was prepared to stand by and help after the hateful struggle was over.

'All right, Bella, I know why you had to open your heart to me. You're in love. I could see it in your face when you first arrived. Are you free to marry?'

'Yes, I am. My husband is dead. An' Henry may be my only chance of happiness. I don't want to lose him, Doc.'

'I see. Well, I'll help all I can, but I can't quite see how. You see, since Jerry changed his plans, I've no means of knowin' where he is. Others may find him before me, an' that won't help you with your plans. But I won't be idle, though. I can see how Jerry has been goin' to the bad for years.

'I'm puzzled, though, that my son should be so cursed with these weaknesses, these afflictions of the flesh. I wonder why he should be like he is? His character doesn't seem to be at all like my own, or that of my late wife.'

Bella thought about the same problem. Perhaps she had a glimmering of the truth. 'I think it may have somethin' to do with your family circumstances. Jerry bein' deprived of his mother at an early age. You bein' engrossed in your work for other people's welfare, an' havin' to be out at all hours.

'Jerry has had a lot of freedom, an' plenty to spend. He's also grown up in a town where his father is idolised, an' that may have made him wild. In any case, you can't be said to have failed him.'

The doctor accepted that crumb of

comfort. He reflected that he, and he only, had to accept the responsibility for the boy. That acceptance was behind everything Bella had said. She had wanted him to act so that others would not put themselves beyond the law. She was asking a lot of him, even though she had at one time almost been a daughter to him.

He shifted his position, set her on her feet, and said, 'Stay the night,' witnessing the dawn of acceptance in the brimming wide-set green eyes.

⋆ ⋆ ⋆

Henry, Bill and Little Ike stayed closer to town than their last camping site. They lay back and smoked for a while, deliberately giving the townsfolk a chance to forget the depth of their feelings when the trio had been forcibly ejected. Inevitably, Henry was the most restless.

'Why don't you jest sink back on the grass there an' stop thinkin' about the whole business for a while?' Bill advised.

'I don't find it all that easy when I know Bella is in there actin' on plans of her own, Bill,' Henry retorted. 'I don't see how any man in my position could be undisturbed. She could run into trouble from the very fellow we're seekin'.'

'Crowds don't react to personable young women the same as they do to men,' Ike expounded. 'They wouldn't hurt her, an' young Rudge couldn't do her any harm unless she found him, which is unlikely. He'd have to catch her in some isolated spot to do her harm. *I* think he'll stay close to people, the ones who sympathise with his Pa all the time.'

'Could be you're right,' Henry admitted.

For a time, he appeared to relax. Upwards of an hour went by during which they all slept, and then Henry was up again and glancing towards the trail and town, wondering if Bella was planning on coming out again. Ike awoke and roused Bill, who looked troubled when he saw the way in which Henry was behaving.

'If you are plannin' on re-entry you'll wait until dark, won't you?' Bill queried.

'I wish I could,' Henry replied, grinning broadly. 'But I can't, because of what might be happenin' in there. I'm goin' in again, real soon.'

Little Ike started to strap up his belongings. Henry saw and scowled. Bill began to do the same. The latter paused, however, as Henry faced them both with his feet apart and pointed his index fingers at them.

'Now see here, boys, I can't take you with me this trip. *I* can slip in unnoticed because I know this town. Three of us can't. Besides, I figure Bella will have gone to the doctor's house for help. Three of us couldn't get near there. It'll take me all my time, seein' as how the Marshal was guardin' the place this mornin'. Besides, we're finally gettin' near to showdown time, an' the showdown is mine, not yours.

'So hold off, if you know what's good for you. If you can't stay away, you wait for darkness. Only don't push me against my will this time, because I won't give.'

Bill argued first, and then Ike. All three were thirsty and hoarse before the two determined henchmen desisted. Henry then thanked them, as he had done before, for their continued loyalty and perseverance on his behalf. He rode part of the way, then dismounted and walked his palomino the rest.

He slipped into town a little to the north of Main and worked his way across to the doctor's residence, having abandoned the palomino in a fenced-off yard at the back of a saloon which had closed through lack of support. Time dragged as he observed the building which was his destination. He waited a long time before he crossed the open ground and set foot upon the shingle drive. There he divested himself of his spurs and began his last surreptitious approach. Working his way in a crouched position, he arrived at the second door. He knocked, and started to relax, and that was his undoing.

Lefty Park was round the nearest corner in a flash. A revolver barrel connected with the side of Henry's head, his senses left him and the deputy dipped a shoulder under him as he collapsed. Park straightened with the intruder's limp body over his shoulder.

Bella opened the door, tried to stifle a scream of anguish, and failed, but all her entreaties failed to move Park. Henry was slung across the deputy's horse. Carrying a double load, it walked rather sedately into town and did not stop until the peace office was reached.

15

In and around town, people began to say bitter things about Henry Walton. They began to be even surer than before that the worst things said about him earlier must have been true; and this was just because he had reentered town after being warned to stay away.

Their anger, however, did not get beyond wordy protests to the Marshal. No one sought to spend the evening raiding the cell block at the back of the office and dragging out the prisoner for the purposes of further injuring him or curtailing his life. Jerry Rudge, at a time when he might have led a new hate campaign, stayed away.

Not so Henry's friends. Little Ike sneaked into town and remained undetected. For a time, he kept a watch on the doctor's house to check whether young Rudge returned there under cover of darkness. Bill Trask acted very boldly. He spent a long time donning his clown's make-up. Soon he was camouflaged in a ginger wig, baggy clothes and white and red paint.

The smell of grease-paint did things to his intelligent mule. It appeared to take in the things which Bill whispered in its ears, and it certainly acted according to his wishes when he led it off towards the town from which it had previously been ejected. This time it had coloured ribbons on its harness and a curious wiggle to the way it walked.

Just short of town, Bill gave it its last instructions, sending it on alone, as if it had broken away from its master. He knew just how it would react, and, in any case, he had no intention of being very far behind. All the way up Main Street, it idled and enchanted the evening strollers, avoiding fondling hands, and, at times, stepping up on to the sidewalk where revellers were more persistent in trying to trap it. Two semi-drunks tried to drop a loop over its head, but their aim was bad, and they attracted as many laughs as the animal, which had the effect of making them desist.

When someone struck up a jolly tune on a honkie-tonk piano, the beast improvised a dance to it, and carried along to a shallow square an admiring following of some fifty people who wanted only to witness something out of the ordinary.

Bill Trask pushed his way through them. One or two of the more discerning spectators identified the mule, and guessed at the identity of its owner, but with Henry Walton safely behind bars they had no qualms over the lesser fry.

Bill went into his regular ring act with the mule, and prolonged it, hoping that in doing so he might materially help one or other of his friends. On the way in, he, like Ike, had heard of Henry's incarceration. He was troubled by this, but not unduly so. For a time, he thought, the initiative was up to Ike, who had hit town before him.

* * *

In his cell, situated at the end of a line of cells off a corridor behind the peace office, Henry fretted and fumed. He had fallen into the hands of those who expressly wanted to turn him from his purpose. Marshal Walker had been along to taunt him, and every time Deputy Park grew bored with haunting the front office, he opened the door to the cell corridor and leered at his prisoner.

Some of the vengeful feeling which Henry felt for Jerry Rudge was transferred to this thick-nosed deputy who was small-minded enough to take great pleasure in another's apparent downfall.

About an hour after dusk, someone tapped on the outer wall of Henry's cell. This happened just after Park had shown his face down the corridor. The prisoner wondered who it was, and rightly judged that it could only be someone who wished him well.

He stood on the board which was his bed and chair. 'All right, who is it? Can't a man have a little privacy even in a cell?'

He sounded like he felt, irritated and out of sorts with himself, and far from being a credit to those who meant most to him.

'It's me, Henry. Ike. I been keepin' a vigil outside the Doc's house, but nothing's happenin'. I heard tell how the deputy picked you up, so I came along to see what was to be done. I guess Bella's in there, spending the night, an' the old man might even have turned in by now. No signs of the young fellow, though. I reckon he's givin' his old man's place the miss jest now.

'Bill's up the street doin' a show with the mule. He has his grease-paint on an' he looks to be busy for quite a while yet. How's it with you?'

'Thanks for gettin' in touch, Ike. I'm stuck for the time bein' an' I can't say I like it. All I can ask you two boys to do is be patient, till I get out again. Think that'll be too much to ask?'

Ike whistled. 'Are you tellin' me you want to *stay* in that cell? That you don't want to be out so's you can take up the hunt again?'

Henry was slow to answer. 'I know you'll do 'most anythin' I ask you, Ike. Above all, I don't want my best friends fouled up in my problems. You've been harried out of town once. I wouldn't want the folks to get mad with you again. So give me a miss, huh? An' sort of keep an unofficial watch on Bella. Give my regards to her, if you see her close, an' to Bill. You all still rate very high with me.'

Outside, Little Ike lost his temper. He fumed and cursed in American and in Spanish, and finally kicked the outer wall of the cell several times. He was breathless when he intimated that he would do what Henry wanted. Before he left, he tossed a twisted piece of wire in through the bars.

When Henry acknowledged this last act, he received no answer. The little man had gone about his business.

For want of something better to do, Henry toyed with the wire. He inserted it in the lock from the cell side. Nothing happened when he tried to open the lock. Still curious, he inserted it from the corridor side, and almost achieved Ike's end. Two small adjustments to the bends in the wire made it a first-class substitute for the real key.

Henry was tempted, and he soon succumbed. He perceived that Ike's efforts were useful ones, and that he had treated the dwarf rather badly. After all, an avenger does not usually allow himself to be incarcerated in a cell on doubtful evidence.

He started to act up almost straight away. 'Hey, Park, how about some food? It ain't so almighty warm that a prisoner can go without sustenance! Show yourself, will you?'

Park was deliberately slow in crossing the office. With a thick smoke between his lips, he came down the corridor and leaned against the door with each of his hands clamped around a bar. He could not have co-operated in a better fashion.

The prisoner moved closer, sticking a boot against the door in case it opened before he was ready.

Park said, 'You'll get food all right, Walton, but not until I'm good an' ready to fetch it, an' I ain't ready yet a while.'

Henry tried to sneer at him, but failed. 'Say, Park, weren't you goin' to be a prize fighter one time? How come a would-be prize fighter has to pistol whip a man instead of using his fists? Can you explain that to me?'

This line of talk soon touched Park on the raw. He felt his misshapen nose, and gripped the bar again, even more fiercely. He started to say, 'If ever you fancy your chances, Walton . . . '

Henry removed his boot, gripped the

bars and pulled. Park was precipitated into the cell. Caught unawares, he ran straight on to Henry's carefully thrown right fist, which stopped his forward progress completely and set him up for the double punch which followed. A left and a right landed on the deputy's jaw with sufficient force to skin the knuckles, but the confounded man dropped easily and made the effort worth while.

He was left locked in the cell without weapons or any aids which could get him out prematurely. Henry left the building by way of the office, collecting his weapons and ducking down an alley to collect the palomino from the rear. He was sorry now that he had not asked Ike to wait.

16

After seeing Henry taken away, Bella could not sleep. She made her peace with the doctor over her sweetheart's having been waylaid by a deputy, and sent the old man to his bed, Rudge submitted readily enough, but his brain was numbed with fears about the possible outcome of the clash between Henry Walton and his son.

In his well-padded bed, he lay back and tried to figure out how he could locate Jerry before Henry did. Even if he succeeded, which was unlikely, he still had to play a major part in his son's downfall; in his punishment for various wrongdoings. The mild potion which he had taken to help him sleep was slow to work on him. Eventually, however, weariness caused him to breathe deeper and slip away from his pressing difficulties.

Sleep eluded Bella altogether. Henry was in jail, but they would not keep him there for ever. He would be back to try again. Doubtless, he would kill Jerry, or die in the attempt. And then there would be the matter of whether the survivor would have a trial to face.

The young woman sat in a wicker chair, looking through the window of the darkened room which had once been her own bedroom. She made certain, for a few moments, that her eyes were not deceiving her when the man who caused her heart to flutter appeared briefly, leading his horse and keeping it quiet by holding its muzzle.

In a flash, she was dressing again, and preparing to do whatever her man wanted of her. She shuddered, thinking that she would be helping him to kill another, and then stiffened her resolve and moved soundlessly through the house to meet him.

At the rear, Henry was doubly cautious, having been caught once. He did not think that the watch would be maintained since he had been thrown into the cell, but he could not be sure. The polished barrel of his .45 was glistening in the light of a faint moon when Bella opened an inner door and catfooted out to join him.

He gasped, and then she did the same. Some of the tension went out of them. They embraced and were slow to come apart.

'How on earth did you get out, darlin'?' Bella whispered.

Henry chuckled. 'Ike threw in a piece of bent wire. I left Park in my place, but sooner or later he'll raise a hullabaloo and then Walker will know I'm at liberty. So I can't stay in such an obvious place for long.'

Bella gripped his hand. 'Come inside,' she pleaded.

Henry hesitated, and when she attempted to draw him along he was slow to follow. 'You want to try an' find clues to Jerry's whereabouts, don't you?' she added hurriedly. 'Well, come an' have a look around while there's still time! I'll keep watch, if it'll make you feel safer!'

Just inside the back door they paused. Henry cleared his throat. 'Bella, you wouldn't let them take me again, for my own good, or any other womanly notion that would keep me from my purpose? Would you?'

'That isn't in my mind, Henry. All I want truly is to have you by me for a few precious minutes before you start huntin' again an' all the awful tension starts again.'

He went in after her then, a little self-conscious about having doubted her. In the back kitchen they came together again. She closed the shutters and drew the drapes. In a low voice, she explained that the doctor was in his bed, and that he definitely had no idea about where to look for Jerry.

Henry pushed back his hat and faced her across the table. 'Are you quite sure about that, Bella? After all, the Doc is his father. A father will do a whole lot for his only son!'

'I'm positive, Henry. I told him all there was to know about Jerry an' why I left Stillwater an' such. He'll help if he has to, but he doesn't know where to look.'

Rasping a thumb along his jaw, Henry became suddenly pensive. He figured that Jerry could not really trust anyone fully except his father, and that meant the son would have to communicate with the doctor. As Jerry was in a tight spot, he would have to think of a subtle method. He said as much.

'He — he may try to contact him tomorrow, when he's out on his rounds,' Bella suggested excitedly.

Henry's interest quickened. 'How about a quick look at the visitin' book?' he suggested.

And that was how they made the discovery. In the daytime, and quite often through the night, the visiting book hung from a nail on the front porch. Bella was the one to fetch it on this occasion. She pushed it into Henry's hands and returned to the front of the house to keep a lookout while he was busy reading through the details.

Doctor Rudge had six calls to make on the following day, but only one of them engaged Henry's attention. It was scribbled in a hand foreign to any he had known. The name given was Jake Smith, who claimed to be a bachelor and a newcomer to the district and to be camping rather roughly near the burned-down shack with the Mex name carved on it. The complaint was stated as being something to do with the stomach.

And that, Henry decided, was all he wanted to know.

If, indeed, the mysterious newcomer was the doctor's son, he himself could diagnose the cause of the stomach complaint. Lack of nourishment. Jerry was keeping so strictly out of the way he hadn't been in a position to lay in food stocks.

Waving the book in his hand, Henry went through to the front of the house and stood with his arm round Bella near a window. Rather hurriedly he explained what he had learned and what his suspicions were. The girl was quietly in agreement with him.

He could feel that she wanted him away now, in case the peace officers came searching for him, and yet she still had something of importance to pass on.

'If I mean anythin' to you, Henry, you'll listen! Don't, I beg you, approach that shack by night. As sure as fate, you'll be picked off. Driven into a corner, Jerry won't hesitate to use his guns on you. So wait, at least until the sun is up. Will you do this for me?'

'All right, I'll do that,' he promised. 'In return, you'll tell Ike an' Bill what I've learned, in the event they come along this way lookin' for me. Is that a bargain?'

'You an' I shouldn't have to make bargains, Henry,' she chided. 'All the same, I'll see the boys are fully informed of the latest developments. So now you must go.'

The alacrity with which he moved caused her mood to change. At the rear of the house she tried to hold him back for a minute or two. He had to assure her that he was only in a hurry to put himself beyond the reach of Marshal Walker before she would release him and move back into the house.

For a mere few seconds, Henry's determination wavered. He was thinking that his whole future was wrapped up in Bella, and that if he called her out again and asked her to go off with him into the night she would do it gladly; provided he forgot about Jerry. And there was the snag, as big and as formidable as ever before. He shrugged away his doubts and quietly collected the palomino, moving off into the night without further pause.

⋆ ⋆ ⋆

For Ike, Bella and Bill, this was a night of little sleep.

The dwarf was quick to hear how

Henry had broken out of jail. He watched men hurrying to the doctor's house, and noted how Bella was able to get rid of Walker and his furious deputy. Several minutes elapsed before the tiny lookout approached the building and was brought up to date by the nervously apprehensive girl.

Bella told Ike what she knew, added her own fears, and asked him to inform Bill of the latest happenings. Reluctantly, she went back indoors, leaving the new chores to friends. On leaving her, Ike searched until he found Bill, and the two of them went into a lengthy discussion about what was best for them to do in the circumstances.

Some time later, they started off towards the remote swale on the south side of the town where the Mexican shack had been located. The moon became contrary, leaving them without sufficient light to make progress over the last mile. This stopped them. After a brief discussion, they made for a knoll on high ground, from which they would be able to see in all directions as soon as it was light.

Without pausing to light a fire, they turned in, rolled in their blankets. Dawn was still scouring the sky when they heard the sound of a single horse's hooves coming from the general direction of town. Hearing the expected noises, Bill sighed with relief. Ike forced a tired grin and started to build a fire.

Their relief, however, was a little premature.

* * *

Bella, on her mare, was ahead of the two lookouts. As the low-lying ground was close to water, the half-mile between her friends and the razed shack was lush with tall grass, blossoming scrub and many stunted pine and oak trees. They failed to see the actual spot, or to see her as she walked the sorrel mare towards the place.

Their failure to be aware of her was largely due to the sudden appearance of

Henry. The hooves they had heard had belonged to his palomino. His approach kept their attention averted from Bella and her destination.

The girl was pale under her tan. Tiny dark smudges under her eyes betrayed the fact that she lacked sleep. Her hands were steady, even so, and her actions those of one totally determined on an odious task. She checked the mare seventy yards short of the razed site and viewed it through thin mist, shuddering when she visualised that awful day when the Mexican child had been burned alive in it. For a few distracting seconds she wondered where the parents were at that very time, and then her mind was firmly fixed on what she had to do.

Through the thinning mist she could see the blackened stubs of walls, and within them the ridged top of a hastily botched-up tent made out of canvas and blankets. Surely, that had to be the hideout of Jeremy Rudge. She entertained the idea that it was all a mistake, and that Jerry had gone on through the town and made good his escape, but some inner feeling made her know beyond any doubt that such was not the case.

Off to westward of her, she could hear sounds which suggested that a small party was breaking camp. She guessed it was her friends. If she hurried, she might come upon Jerry still tucked up in his blanket, and she was prepared to threaten him with a revolver to get him to clear out before the showdown. This, she thought, was her best course of action.

With her knees, she urged the reluctant mare forward. It had not relished being made to work before dawn. After turning its head and bestowing upon her one more glance of disapproval, it started forward again. Bella licked her lips. She pulled the highly-polished Colt which had once been part of her shooting act, and thumbed back the hammer.

Thirty yards from the tent, she

noticed the canvas move, but this was only caused by a light breeze. She was still staring at it when Jerry's voice took her by surprise. He was about twenty-five yards farther east than the tent and the shack, hunkered behind a fallen log masked by scrub. The business end of his rifle stared at her like a black and baleful eye.

'Be careful, Bella,' he warned in a dry, tense voice. 'We both know how good you are with that gun, an' we both know I'll use this rifle if I have to. So why don't you toss down that fancy weapon an' start comin' towards me, huh?'

The girl bit her lip. 'Do you really think you could shoot me an' then face your father afterwards, Jerry, after I spent the night at his house?'

'If that's what you have in mind, don't try any tricks! Now, do as I say, if you don't want to cause a second tragedy at this spot!'

Bella retorted: 'You wouldn't want to kill two females at the same place, would you?' But she moved steadily in his direction, after discarding her gun.

Jerry rose up and beckoned her round the scrub, always keeping his rifle trained on her body. He moved close enough to grab her reins, and then he started to relax a little, although his lined countenance showed that the strain was telling on him rather badly.

'An' now we can prepare for further visitors. I figure if you knew where I was, Henry will know, too. That means he'll be here ahead of Pa, an' that surely ain't healthy for any of you! Hold still while I mount up.'

He manoeuvred the mare nearer to his waiting dun, and achieved the saddle without mishap. Bella had been distracted by the sounds of horses moving up to the site of the ruined shack. She was aware of a slight hesitation in her captor's mind, and then he was urging dun and mare towards the narrow track above the shack.

Together, they became aware of Henry coming towards them. Bill and Ike, whom he had recently joined, were a few yards to the rear, but backing him watchfully. Henry was quick to raise his arm and check his followers. Rudge laughed. He had put away his rifle and was controlling the proceedings with a six-gun, the muzzle of which was pushed into Bella's side.

'All right, Walton, so you've seen an' read the sign. We're comin' right through you, an' if either of your sidekicks or you make a false move, she dies! I'm sure I make myself clear!'

Henry's tongue appeared to be stuck to the roof of his mouth. His friends were also stunned into silence. One after the other, they holstered their guns and made way for the hated man and the threatened girl. Some little distance nearer town, the latest-comer checked his bay horse with a firm hand, and awaited developments.

Such was the tension between the five people ahead of him that none of them was immediately aware of his presence. The doctor was also muted by what he saw, but his hands were busy, nevertheless. He witnessed his son making his way through the trio of his enemies, using the girl as a guarantee of his own safety. It was confirmed to the doctor, in that instant, that he loved the girl more than his own son.

Jerry achieved his immediate purpose and started to draw away from the tense trio, sided by the mare and the stiff-backed girl. When they were twenty yards clear, the captor suddenly pulled the gun away from the girl, lined it up on his enemy and pulled the trigger. Henry was too close for him to miss. With a strangled cry, the victim lurched in the saddle, swung sideways and pitched to the trail.

Bill and Ike braved the threat of the gun, hurriedly dismounting and moving to tend their friend. Bella pivoted in the saddle, saw what had happened and at once lost control of herself. She lashed out with a boot, kicking the dun away from the mare, and thereby precipitating the next move.

Doctor Rudge's gun boomed before

either Bella or Jerry had seen him. He had waited only for Bella to be a safe distance from Jerry before firing his weapon. His bullet ploughed into Jerry's skull just above the level of his hatband, entering his brain and cutting off life.

As Jerry hit the dust, Bella merely blinked. She managed to become mobile again as the buckboard came up with her. Side by side, a few moments later, she and the doctor checked over Henry's wound. It was high in his right shoulder. By sheer will power she fought off faintness, waiting to hear the diagnosis.

'Bella, my dear, Henry will be all right. He won't take any great harm. Moreover, I'll see the record is straightened in regard to his all-time innocence!'

The doctor sighed, and the two willing helpers grabbed the girl as she fainted away with relief. The old man was suffering more than it showed. He had a feeling that the faint trickle of water on the lower ground would one day have the name of Killer's Creek.

Other titles in the Linford Western Library:

HELL'S COURTYARD

Cobra Sunman

Indian Territory, popularly called Hell's Courtyard, was where bad men fled to escape the law. Buck Rogan, a deputy marshal hunting the killer Jed Calder, found the trail leading into Hell's Courtyard and went after his quarry, finding every man's hand against him. Rogan was also searching for the hideout of Jake Yaris, an outlaw running most of the lawlessness directed at Kansas and Arkansas. Single-minded and capable, Rogan would fight the bad men to the last desperate shot.

SARATOGA

Jim Lawless

Pinkerton operative Temple Bywater arrives in Saratoga, Wyoming facing a mystery: who murdered Senator Andrew Stone? Was it his successor, Nathan Wedge? Or were lawyers Forrest and Millard Jackson, and Marshal Tom Gaines involved? Bywater, along with his sidekick Clarence Sugg, and Texas Jack Logan, faces gunmen whose allegiances are unknown. The showdown comes in Saratoga. Will he come out on top in a bloody gun fight against an adversary who is not only tough, but also completely unforeseen?

PEACE AT ANY PRICE

Chap O'Keefe

Jim Hunter and Matt Harrison's Double H ranch thrived . . . till their crew marched away to war's glory, and outlaws destroyed everything and murdered oldster Walt Burridge. When the war ended, the two Hs started over. However, for Jim, war had wrought changes beyond endurance. So Jim rode out and into the arms of his wartime love, the gun-running adventuress Lena-Marie Baptiste. Now, trapped by his vow to avenge Old Walt, he must choose between enmity and love, life and death.

SIX DAYS TO SUNDOWN

Owen G. Irons

When his horse is shot dead, Casey Storm is forced to brave a high plains blizzard. Stumbling upon a wagon train of Montana settlers, he helps them to fight their way toward the new settlement of Sundown. But gunmen hired by a land-hungry madman follow. Now the wagon train's progress seems thwarted by their pursuers and the approaching winter. With only six bloody days to reach Sundown, will Casey's determination win through to let them claim their land?

MISTAKEN IN CLAYMORE RIDGE

Bill Williams

Ben Oakes had always been involved in trouble — he'd killed men before — but now he was determined to live a new life and never to carry a weapon. But when he's wrongfully imprisoned for the murder of Todd Hakin, he's desperate to clear his name and escape the hangman's noose. Then Ben is finally released, and his search for Todd's killer leads him to Claymore Ridge, where he faces threats to his life from more than one quarter . . .